The Animals' Lawsuit Against Humanity

The Animals' Lawsuit Against Humanity

A Modern Adaptation of an Ancient Animal Rights Tale

Translated and adapted by
Rabbi Anson Laytner and Rabbi Dan Bridge

Edited by Matthew Kaufmann

Introduced by Seyyed Hossein Nasr

Illustrated by Kulsum Begum

FONS VITAE

First published in 2005 by
Fons Vitae
49 Mockingbird Valley Drive
Louisville, KY 40207
http://www.fonsvitae.com

Printed in China by Everbest Co. Ltd.,
through Four Colour Imports, Ltd.•Louisville, Kentucky

Library of Congress Control Number: 2005920649

ISBN 1-887752-70-6

Publication of this book was funded in part
by a technical assistance grant
from the Kongsgaard-Goldman Foundation.

This book was typeset by Neville Blakemore, Jr.

CONTENTS

DEDICATIONS

To my wife, Merrily, for all her love and support;
and to my children, Miriam, Anna, and Amy,
and my children's children, for they shall inherit the earth.

Anson Laytner

To my sons, Jacob and Zachary, who teach me daily wonders
of creation.

Dan Bridge

ACKNOWLEDGEMENTS

Deepest gratitude for making this book possible goes to a wonderful and caring woman in Kentucky whose life and heart are devoted to our environment and the sanctity of animal life.

We would like to thank the following people for their advice, editorial suggestions, and encouragement:

Janine Skolnik Benton, Shoshanna Brown, Martha Kongsgaard, Lindy Orlin, Carole Hosford, Elizabeth Wales, and Claire Vardiel Zaslove.

PREFACE

A Note to the Reader about this Tale

How often does one come across a thousand-year old "animal rights" tale, written first in Arabic by Muslims, then translated into Hebrew by a Jew at the request of a medieval Christian king, and now translated into English and adapted by two Jews and a Christian, and illustrated by a Muslim lady from Pakistan in the employ of a Saudi princess? Read on...

I

The volume itself was a small Hebrew paperback, printed on cheap, browning newsprint, and published in Jerusalem under the title *Iggeret Baalei Hayyim* (*The Letter of the Animals*) by Mosad HaRav Kook in 1949. I happened upon it some twenty years ago while wandering the stacks in the library of the Hebrew Union College in Cincinnati where I was doing research for my rabbinic thesis/book *Arguing with God: A Jewish Tradition*. At the time, all I knew was that the story involved a dispute between people and animals at the Court of the King of the Spirits over humanity's alleged abuse of these creatures. Although it was beyond the scope of my then-current work, I was nonetheless fascinated by the timeliness of its plot and its multi-faith authorship.

So I photocopied the small paperback, filed it away, and took it with me when I graduated. It traveled with me to Larchmont, New York, and later, to Seattle, Washington, where it sat untouched for twelve years. In the due course of time, my friend and colleague, Dan Bridge, and I decided to become study partners in order to deepen our Hebrew skills and Jewish knowledge. Only then did I recall the story that I had filed away so long before. Thus it was, on almost every Friday morning, for nearly two years, we would meet to translate a portion of *Iggeret Baalei Hayyim* (*The Letter of the Animals*). During the week, I would enter our work on the computer. Much later, when we had finished translating, we began to polish and edit, to revise and rewrite. Still later, I continued adapting the work on my own, receiving advice from many individuals who were interested in seeing the story published. When I began to seek a publisher for the tale, a friend suggested Fons Vitae because of its focus on spiritual texts and inter-faith dialogue. The publisher, Gray Henry, is a Kentuckian and something of a free spirit with a great love of Islamic mysticism. She became as enthusiastic as I was about the tale's lesson and its history. Both were important messages for our day and age. Gray asked Matthew Kaufmann, a Christian and then a student at Bellarmine University, to do a final edit of the tale and to add additional color and texture to the story.

II

Our work marks the first time that the Hebrew edition has been translated into English, albeit in a more readable and dramatic form. But that too is in keeping with its history. In actuality, the antecedents of the story were Indian, but the first written version of the story was penned in Arabic by members of the Islamic "Order of the Pure Brethren", a Sufi order, in the environs of Basra, Iraq, sometime during the tenth century of the Common Era. In their version, the story was the twenty-fifth of fifty-one "letters", or treatises, comprising an encyclopedia, which described the mysteries and meaning of life.

Much later, this one story, *The Letter of the Animals*, was translated and adapted (in seven days, no less!) by Rabbi Kalonymus ben (son of) Kalonymus, known among Christians as Maestro Calo, at the request of his master, King Charles of Anjou (in France), in the year 1316 of the Common Era. Even Kalonymus' telling of the tale apparently exists in several widely differing versions—compare the Hebrew text upon which this story is based with the version cited by Morris Epstein in his introductory essay to *Mishle Sendebar*, (*The Tales of Sendebar*), (Jewish Publication Society, 1967), in which the case is argued before the King of the Birds, not the King of the Spirits. The story was popular in European Jewish communities into the late 19th and early 20th centuries. Besides being published in Hebrew, it also was translated into Yiddish, German and Spanish.

As a story type, this work bears similarities to the 12th century Sufi fable *The Conference of the Birds*, by Farid ud-Din Attar. Indeed, in the version cited by Epstein in his introduction to *Mishle Sendebar*, the beasts take their complaint before the sovereign of the birds. Comparable stories from other cultures include the 18th century Japanese philosophical satire *The Animal Court* by Ando Shoeki and *The Animals' Conference* by Erich Kastner, a post World War II fable about making peace "for children and other understanding people".

III

The tale as we present it is but a highly adapted fraction of the original whole, the ingenious kernel that first caught my fancy. The original tale itself is much longer, with numerous philosophical and theological digressions, and tales within tales. We found it necessary to sacrifice a number of these in order to highlight the essential story. In our version, we gave the characters symbolic names and a touch of personality, whereas in the original the humans, in particular, were nameless and generally offensive ethnic stereotypes—and all male besides!

We also decided to significantly embellish the ending by giving the King a major speech before he announces his verdict and by dramatically heightening the importance of his judgment for our own time. Even so, we believe our ending remains true to the intent of Kalonymus' version. We also chose, in a moment of multi-faith whimsy, to base King Bersaf's final speech on passages from the *Tao Te Ching*. As in the Hebrew version of the tale, our story concludes with a poem that recapitulates the broad outlines of the story. However, for our version, I chose to write my own poem rather than simply translate the original.

A word about "spirits". The Jerusalem Talmud divides these variously named beings into three types: *mazzikim* (harmful spirits), *shedim* (good or bad spirits) and *ruhot* (spirits which can possess a person). In the Babylonian Talmud—from the country in which this story originated—the world was thought to be filled with all sorts of spirits. "If the eye could see them, no one could endure the spirits (*mazzikim*)...They are more numerous than we are and they surround us...Every person has a thousand on his left and ten thousand on his right..." (Berachot 6a). The Ramban (Nachmanides), a 13th century Spanish rabbi, scholar and mystic, claimed that spirits were not created out of the four elements, but rather only from fire and air, allowing them to fly through air. However, like human beings, they were subject to both life and death, even though their longevity was greater. In our story, the word we translate as "spirits" is *shedim*. We could have translated them as "demons" but that seemed too prejudicial a term, given the negative connotations the word has in English. We also considered substituting the Arabic word *djinn* as in "genie" for "spirit" or "demon" but, thanks to Aladdin—and Disney—that is an equally loaded word. The important point to remember is that whether called "spirits", "demons", *djinn*, or "genie", these beings are benevolent, wise and devout.

At the conclusion of the tale, I have added a short essay on the spiritual value of treating animals—and indeed all of Creation—lovingly and with compassion. I have also included a smattering of quotes from Jewish traditions supporting the importance of this principle—in case the objective evidence of the decline of our natural world needs any reinforcement.

At any rate, we hope you will forgive our *chutzpah* for making the changes we have made, but it is our hope that, by bringing a "lost classic" to a new generation in a new land, our retelling of this story both will rescue a wonderful tale from obscurity and at the same time invigorate our collective efforts at *tikkun olam*, the repair of the world.

Anson Laytner
Tu b'Shevat 5765
25 January, 2005

May the multi-faith coöperation that informed the transmission of this tale and the publishing of this version of it inspire people of faith everywhere—and in the Middle East in particular—to overcome their theological differences and recognize their overwhelming similarities in order to work together for the common good of humankind and other living creatures.

This volume is dedicated to the hope that the time will come when we humans treat all sentient beings with compassion and respect.

INTRODUCTION

In the mid 1950's when writing my doctoral thesis at Harvard on Islamic concepts of nature and cosmology in the 4th /10th century, I decided to devote the first part of the work to the *Epistles (Rasa'il)* of the Ikhwan al-Safa' or the Brethren of Purity. While going over the Arabic text I was struck at the same time by the beauty and the timeliness and contemporary significance of the treatise on the dispute between man and the animals in part two of the *Rasa'il*, a treatise dealing with the complaints of animals to the king of the *jinn* because of their mistreatment at the hands of the children of Adam. The message of the story appeared to me to be particularly timely because even then there was a keen intuition in my mind concerning the impending crisis in man's relation with nature, a subject to which I turned a decade later in my *Man and Nature*, written at the dawn of general awareness of what came to be known as the ecological and later environmental crisis. My thesis appeared in print in 1964 as *An Introduction to Islamic Cosmological Doctrines* and this work turned the attention of a number of scholars to the story of the dispute between man and the animals.

The story had been generally neglected in twentieth century Western scholarship although it was translated by J. Platts into English in the nineteenth century as *Dispute between Man and the Animals* and by F. Dieterici into German as part of his translation of the *Rasa'il*. One of the scholars whose attention was turned to this story as a result of reading my book on Islamic cosmology was Lynn Goodman who then translated the text into English again as *The Case of Animals versus Man Before the King of Jinn*. There is also a contemporary German translation of the story entitled *Mensch und Tiervor den König der Dschinnen* by A. Giese.

The destiny of this work during the Middle Ages remained, however, neglected. It is interesting to note that this work was very popular in its Hebrew version among Jewish scholars who played such an important role in the transmission of Islamic learning in the Middle Ages to the Latin West. It is perhaps even more interesting to note that this story was translated into Latin for a Christian king in France, Charles of Anjou, by a Jewish scholar. Like so much of the philosophy and science of the medieval period in Spain, this remarkable tale bears the mark of an Abrahamic cooperation, one in whose creation and propagation Muslims, Jews and Christians participated. It is, therefore, a doubly significant work as far as the contemporary world is concerned, for it is first of all concerned with man's relation to animals and more generally to the natural environment, and secondly it is rooted in an ecumenical perspective which permitted the Islamic treatment of the subject to be also adopted and appreciated by Jewish and Christian scholars and more general readers.

The essential message of this wonderful tales negates completely that concept of man based on hubris and pride which enables modern human beings to utilize, dominate and destroy other species always with the pretext of fulfilling so-called human needs, making the rights of man over other creatures absolute. Needless to say this egocentrism and hubris have always existed but it became especially emphasized in the West with Renaissance humanism and the idealization what I have elsewhere called Promethean man. What is most significant in this treatise is that all the arguments bought up by man to justify his domination and abuse of animals are countered and negated by various animals as they defend their case before the king of the *jinn*. There remains but one reason for man's superiority that the animals cannot refute and that is the possibility of a number among men to attain sanctity and therefore to be able to act as the channel of the grace for the rest of God's creation. But to fulfill this function of being truly the vice-regent of God on earth (*Khalifat Allah fi'l-ard*), as the Quran describes the function of the human being here on earth, means to overcome that very hubris and self-aggrandizement which are the source of abuse of the rest of God's creation and about which the animals were complaining before the king of the *jinn* in the first place.

This story, although a thousand years old, brings up issues of the greatest contemporary significance as far as the environmental crisis is concerned. What are our rights over other creatures and what are the limits of their rights? What about the rights of animals? What is the goal of human life and what is our role vis-à-vis the rest of God's creation while we seek to attain that goal? These are questions of momentous import at a time when human beings have adopted modes of living totally out of harmony with the natural environment and a way of life based on complete disregard for the life of other creatures, a way of life which has made modern human beings an endangering and at the same time an endangered species.

This story can be an important source for the formulation of a contemporary Islamic environmental philosophy, a philosophy whose expression in current language is a dire necessity for the Islamic world, which, like other parts of the world, is suffering from serious environmental problems. But this story can also provide food for thought for Jewish and Christian thinkers involved in environmental issues and the formulation of Jewish and Christian theologies of nature and environmental philosophies. Moreover, the history of this tale, written in Iraq by Muslims, translated into Hebrew by Jews, and rendered into Latin for a Christian king—not to speak of joint "Abrahamic" coöperation in the preparation of the present book—remind us of the basic truth that the most crucial problems of today are those which all authentic religious people face together. How much better it would be for all humanity if, rather than facing each other in contention, the religions would live in harmony and join their resources in facing the excruciating problems of the day—among the most important being the environmental crisis—problems that threaten earthly human existence itself?

Fons Vitae is to be congratulated in making this work in its current form, which reflects directly the coöperation of representatives from all of the religions of the Abrahamic family, available in the English language. They have provided a book of value for experts on medieval thought as well as ordinary readers interested in reading a fascinating story of enduring spiritual worth and great current significance.

Seyyed Hossein Nasr
November , 2004
Ramadan, 1425 (A.H.)

xiv

The Animals' Lawsuit Against Humanity

LIST OF MAJOR CHARACTERS

Humans	Animals
Ahzar (Cruelty)	Camel
Ga'avah (Pride)	Cow
Hasad (Jealousy)	Cricket
Hochmah (Wisdom)	Donkey
Ka'as (Anger)	Dragon
Kasal (Sloth)	Elephant
Shabakah (Lust)	Frog
Shara (Gluttony)	Horse
Tama (Greed)	Mule
Tawadu (Humility)	Nightingale
Unf (Violence)	Ox
Zadone (Malice)	Parrot
	Pig
	Queen Bee
	Sheep

Spirits

Bersaf (King of the Spirits)

Peruz (Advisor to the King)

GATE ONE

The enslavement of the beasts by the humans and
how the beasts brought suit against humanity in the
Court of Bersaf, King of the Spirits

I

Long, long ago, there was a place on earth where the animals lived
alone, free from persecution by human beings. That was the island
of Tsagone, in the middle of the Green Sea, right on the heart of the
equator. The island was in the Kingdom of the Spirits, and it was
an enchanted isle, ruled by Bersaf, King of the Spirits. No human
has ever visited this island, either before or after the story you are
about to hear.

Tsagone was a magical place, alive with various trees and fruits,
grasses, seeds and flowers. The air was moist with gentle fra-
grance—not a single scent or spice was missing. All the different
species of animals dwelled there, those with cloven hooves and those
without; a seemingly endless spectrum of birds; animals of prey
and beasts of the field; and every kind of flying and creeping insect.
All lived together in peace: the wolf and the lamb, the tiger and the
goat, the cow and the bear, the eagle and the turtle dove. The wild
donkey, the deer, the antelope, and the birds of prey, together with
those they now eat, all lived together in happiness and contentment;
their young danced in joy before them. They knew nothing of fear,
and were fortunate enough not learn of violence or greed. There
was no hostility or trouble—no grudges, no hatred, no enmity—
only peace and neighborliness, love and common-animality.

One day, a large wooden ship happened to be traveling in the Green
Sea *en route* to Massah. On board were people of every faith and
custom, representing each of the seventy nations of the world: men
and women; merchants and knights; artisans and artists; storekeepers and doctors; farmers and seekers of wisdom. A terrible storm

One day, a large wooden ship happened to be traveling in the Green Sea en route to Massah. On board were people of every faith and custom, representing each of the seventy nations of the world: men and women; merchants and knights; artisans and artists; storekeepers and doctors; farmers and seekers of wisdom. A terrible storm arose on their journey, as quickly and unexpectedly as death can introduce itself into one's life. The sea would rise and fall, tower and plummet. Unmerciful waters would pound the ship with relentless power. The sailors rowed for their lives, but were unable to prevail against the anger of the sea.

arose on their journey, as quickly and unexpectedly as death can introduce itself into one's life. The sea would rise and fall, tower and plummet. Unmerciful waters would pound the ship with relentless power. The sailors rowed for their lives, but were unable to prevail against the anger of the sea. The ship began to fill with water and foundered near the island. Fortunately, by evening, the wind turned gentle and cast them safely onto the shores of the green island of Tsagone. The boat, however, was destroyed, and would never sail again.

Once ashore, they turned their eyes to Heaven and gave thanks, in their multitude of ways, for their salvation from the fury of the storm. Then they set out to explore the island. There they saw many kinds of trees and fruits and grasses growing in its fertile soil; they tasted its sweet waters and savored the pleasant evening weather; the colorful flowers alive with beauty and the fragrant spices laced with inspiration filled the peoples' hearts with joy. They also observed all the animals living together in peace and marveled at such a sight.

"We must be the first human beings ever to set foot on this island! Look how unafraid the animals are of us!"

"This is truly paradise," agreed another. "It is by the grace of God that we have landed here safely. We are in the land of innocence!"

"Yes indeed," declared a third, a greedy man by the name of Tama. "Here's a golden opportunity if I ever saw one. We can be kings here! We can rule this place, and make our own way. God blesses us!"

Realizing there was no known method for them to leave the enchanted isle, the people decided to make the best of things. They built houses and planted crops, established a town and set up markets on every corner. But not everyone was content with this situation.

"We work too hard," complained Kasal, stifling a yawn. "Back home, we had servants and slaves to do our bidding. We had animals to plow and animals to carry—who are we going to find here to do all this labor? I thought we were going to be kings."

"Why just sit there and whine?" demanded Zadone, "Let's grab some of these animals and put them to use. Not only can they work for us, but we can eat them to sustain ourselves." Hochmah, a wise woman, replied to Zadone with a tone of reverence in her voice, "But we must be careful not to build our society around the avoidance of hard work and the growling of our stomachs. We have a chance to create a new culture here, one that can truly elevate the quality of life for all of us. We mustn't abuse these animals or we will be abusers. The consequences of such self-centered intentions are inevitable destruction of the life within and around us."

Few ears could understand these words, but a few humble people absorbed them with transforming feelings. Unfortunately, the focus on freedom from labor and the possibility of meat to eat took hold of most of the minds and hearts of the crowd. This focus intoxicated the crowd in a hypnotic desire, and Zadone knew this. He spoke briefly to Hochmah, 'We won't be abusers. They won't know the difference—they're nothing but dumb animals. We'll choose the kind of life they live and they'll get used to it!" Zadone then turned to the crowd, "We will have our slaves! We will build our kingdom *our* way!"

The crowd erupted with applause; birds flew from the trees in fear.

"We'll have all the animals we need in no time," declared Ahzar.

"Why should we suffer when they can do so much for us? They are nothing. They are meant for our pleasure." added Unf.

Ahzar stood to his feet yelling to the crowd, "Arm yourselves! The hunt has begun. Grab your weapons, and join us!" The crowd shouted with fever! The floor shook as the men left for the hunt with thirsting enthusiasm. Tiny bugs observed the men with curious expressions of wonder.

Capturing the animals proved easier than they had expected. The animals had never met any humans before and thus had no reason to fear them, no reason to hide, no reason to abandon their state of innocence. The animals looked to the men with eyes alive with trust, and thus they were easily taken advantage of by the humans.

The men captured some of the cloven-hoofed animals—sheep, cattle and camels—and some of the beasts—horses, mules and donkeys—and bound them tightly with rough ropes and put bridles in their mouths, and forced them to work. The people used them for riding, carrying, plowing and pulling heavily laden wagons. Others they took and slaughtered so that they could eat meat once again. The animals watched with fear as their brothers and sisters were slaughtered, cooked, and eaten. The humans treated the animals with great cruelty, pushing them beyond their endurance, just as they had done with animals in their own lands.

At first, the animals did not know what evil had befallen them, but soon they realized their whole way of life had changed for the worse. Eyes that were once filled with trust began to be drowned in stormy oceans of fear. Some animals were able to flee far away, to distant deserts and deep dark valleys, to thick forests and high mountains. But the people pursued them and recaptured most of them. Animals that once walked the earth in freedom began to feel the unexpected pain of sharp metal traps clutching their feet as they walked with trusting steps. Some learned not to walk so trustingly, and were able to survive; others were caught and forced to return to the life into which the humans had compelled them. The ground that once gave them pleasure now rose up and attacked them with new methods of violence. The animals could only wait in pain, submitting to their fate, and returned to their life of slavery.

"You animals are our slaves—How dare you attempt to flee from us!" Ga'avah exclaimed with wounded pride. And Ka'as shouted out in anger: "Ahzar, Unf—show them what we do with rebels." Ahzar stared at the horse with merry, evil eyes. He whipped the horse as the horse whinnied in pain. The horse looked with a searching expression for someone to help him, but the people just laughed and pointed at him. Unf spit in his face. The horse had no choice but to accept the abuse. He lowered his head, and felt the whip that once stung his skin now make his skin numb. The hearts of Ahzar and Unf danced with joy at their savagery.

When the animals still living in freedom learned about the fate of the captives, they gave thanks to their Creator for their survival, and then took secret counsel together in a remote part of the island.

"Running away won't help," Horse neighed, "We tried that but they pursued us and managed to recapture many. Besides, they never give up the chase. We will always be hunted. They don't see us as free living creatures, they see us as slaves and as food."

"It's true," moaned Cow, "And so many of us are injured. They set traps all around us so that we can't even walk without fear. Look at my leg, it won't stop bleeding."

"How can they treat us so cruelly? We have done nothing to them." lowed Ox in despair. "I just want our old life back. I miss my family, I'm afraid I'll never see them again."

"We should ask Bersaf the King of the Spirits for help," suggested Mule. "He is a wise and noble spirit who knows the value of justice."

"Is it possible?" asked Cow.

Mule put his head next to Cow's, "It is if you have faith. We must believe this way of life was not meant for us."

"Justice!" exclaimed Ox. He shouted again and again, "Justice! Justice! We deserve justice!" And the beasts began to chant together. A slow rumble turned into a towering thunder of voices, "Justice! Justice! Justice!" Their hearts began to rise as they felt the solidarity of their purpose; hope began to ascend in their eyes, and they ventured off to the King's Court together.

But none of them had even seen a spirit. And no creature of flesh and blood had ever been to the Spirit King's Court.

Yet they knew the Palace existed, as did the spirit kingdom, as did the spirits themselves. They sensed the spirits, felt their joy and heard their wisdom whispering in the howling winds. They knew of stories that proclaimed spirits taking on physical forms in order to communicate to those living who walked the land.

Mule spoke to his friends, "Let us call to the spirits! Let us call together in one voice! Everyone! Shout with your heart through your lips!"

The animals stood in a circle, facing outwards, and brayed and lowed, bleated and neighed, until the air began to quiver and shimmy. Soon, all around them, changing shapes and visages began to dance, fading in and out before their tearing eyes. In the midst of all this, Bersaf the Wise, King of the Spirits, Ruler of the Island of Tsagone, appeared, flickering first as a being, bug-eyed, bewhiskered and bristling with lightening; then as crackling energy, cat's eyes and canine teeth; and then as a serene face, neither human nor animal, set amid the reds and oranges of a setting sun.

The beasts were filled with awe and dread. They fell on their faces before him, weeping, and told him all that had befallen them. Voices cried out in desperation, and fell silent in unison when Mule explained, "Our lives have been stolen by the violence of these humans! We are the victims of all their anger, ignorance, and laziness! Please help us... We beg for your mercy..."

And King Bersaf the Wise, pure and honest, God-fearing and shunning evil, hospitable to guests, a defender of the poor, merciful toward the unfortunate, a dispenser of gifts and charity, far-removed from oppression, despising iniquity, opposing villainy with great conviction and with great anger—there isn't another like him in all creation!— grew green with inner rage as he heard their sad tale.

"No life should undergo such abuse. These humans have lost sight of the life within you." King Bersaf raised his voice, his eyes beamed with empathy, "I feel your sorrow and your loss... It is an outrage against our Creator that these humans treat you animals so cruelly! I will confront these humans in my court! Justice will be realized!"

II

So the King of the Spirits sent messengers to the people ordering them to come before him to account for the oppression and violence that they were alleged to have done.

The people were distraught. Until then they were in the habit of thinking that they were the lords of all. And now, suddenly, as if awakened from a deep dream, they found themselves accountable

11

THE ANIMALS' LAWSUIT AGAINST HUMANITY

for what they had done and were doing. Immediately they split into two parties. One group was already upset, troubled by the cruelty they had seen done to the innocent animals, and sad to see the island paradise disrupted. They spoke amongst themselves, seemingly random voices arising from the crowd.

"How could we be so unaware of the violence we do?"

"Maybe the king's action will help by forcing us all to realize our better nature?"

"The responsibility for our hearts is ours to see."

But the other group, led by Ga'avah, Ka'as and Zadone, was stronger. Though the two parties argued, in the end the latter group always won—Unf and Ahzar made sure of that with their constant intimidation. Speaking loudly and refusing to listen, they closed their hearts and their minds off from any view that did not support their agendas.

Hochmah, the female sage, spoke amongst all the people: "It makes no sense to have treated the animals so harshly. They were practically tame to begin with. Now your activities have landed us in trouble with the ruler of this realm! I do not want your violence associated with my way of life. I tried to warn you before. Violence is barbaric! And we are capable of so much more. We can live our lives in peace." A number of people nodded their heads in agreement—until Ahzar, Unf and their followers stepped forward, crowding the breath of the people with their angry and disapproving looks.

"Please listen," soothed Zadone slyly with a calming smile, "Perhaps some of us *did* go too far in the beginning, but after all, the situation was desperate when we first came ashore. That was *then*. But this is now—what good will it do for us to present a divided front at the King's Court? We need to stand together or we'll all lose our homes, our farms, everything. The King needs to see that we live in harmony together. We have no other choice."

Intimidated and apparently out-numbered, the wise woman Hochmah and her circle reluctantly agreed to go along with the others, knowing deep down that they forfeited the actions of their understandings to people with evil intentions. They buried their feelings of responsibility and guilt by convincing themselves that they didn't have a choice.

So they sent seventy chosen people to the King's Court, representing all languages, faiths and nations of the earth, each dressed according to the custom of his or her own land.

They traveled, as commanded, to the very center of the island that was dominated by a single, snow-capped volcano. There, at its summit, partially obscured by dense white clouds and misty steam, rose a palace of red and gold and black. Its surface was so pure and shiny that the light reflected off of the palace's walls nearly blinded many humans. Its columns—so it seemed to them—appeared insubstantial; they quivered and shimmered behind their moist veil of sparkling steam. They wondered how the pillars could hold up the magnificent golden tiled roof. The light seemed to embrace the palace, expanding and contracting from it in a surrounding sphere. It appeared to be breathing. As they drew closer, they were spotted by the King's servants, who announced the arrival of the humans to their Spirit Master.

When the humans were ushered into the audience hall, King Bersaf chose to appear as the serene, red-orange face of the sun-being; then as crackling energy, flashing cat's eyes and snarling canine teeth; and lastly as a glaring, bug-eyed and bewhiskered monster bristling with lightening.

As anticipated, the human delegation stopped dead in its tracks when it saw this fearsome display. Huddling together, they advanced slowly until they stood before this presence and, bowing low, they declaimed together in a loud voice the words they had rehearsed: "May our Lord the King live long; may his years be good and his days pleasant! We are very pleased to be invited here before him."

But the King was not pleased. He demanded an explanation from them: "Why have you seized and oppressed these pitiful beasts? Why do you abuse them? Have you no respect for life?!" His voice reverberated through the palace, echoing throughout the land. The ground beneath the humans' feet trembled, and they recognized fear in each others' eyes.

Zadone, the spokesperson for the people, centered himself and stood to confront the task before him. He looked downcast as if to suggest that it pained him more than it did the animals to treat them so badly. He replied with careful words, "The truth is, my Lord and King, that these and all other animals are our slaves and that we are their masters. We own them. But some of these animals rebelled against us and fled from their work. That cannot be allowed, as I'm sure you can understand, my Lord. So we pursued them, recaptured those we could and disciplined them. There's really nothing more to it than that, Your Highness. As you know, a society without some form of discipline is one of chaos, and we endeavor to live a life within order. So, wise King, please judge between us and these, our slaves, who have sinned by rebelling against us. May God direct your noble heart in the path of truth and justice."

As he spoke, the King gradually was mollified. When Zadone finished, the King was inclined to listen to both sides and inquired: "What evidence do you have that they are your slaves?"

Ga'avah, a pretty woman, strode proudly forward and declared in a voice rich with reading: "God raised us human beings over all other creatures and gave us the animals and other foods to eat, as God said to Adam and Eve: 'Fill the earth and master it, rule the fish of the sea, the birds of the sky and all the living things that creep on earth.' And God also said to Noah: 'The fear and the dread of you shall be upon all the beasts of the earth and upon all the birds of the sky and every creature that lives shall be yours to eat.' All this proves that God created animals solely for our use. They are our slaves and we are their masters. Justice is on our side."

The King turned to the animals and asked: "Do you have an answer to this human's words?"

Mule arose and said: "My Lord, I will refute her words. This human has not offered a single proof to support the notion that they are our masters and we are their slaves. God created humans from dust and ashes and put them on earth to dwell on it, but not to destroy it; to coexist with us, the other living creatures, and to obtain benefit from us, but not to oppress us—and certainly not to kill us!

The sun and moon, the clouds and the wind also give humans benefit. Does this mean that they too are humanity's servants? Animals provide benefit to the humans and help them in many ways, that's true; but it was never the Creator's intent that the humans be our masters and we their slaves, or that they should treat us so cruelly. To think this way is the height of pride!"

Donkey spoke up: "Our Lord and King, our ancestors dwelt in this land even before Adam and Eve were created. We dwelled in all its corners and roamed freely, busying ourselves with raising our young and providing food for them. Then these humans arrived on this island and they began to make our lives miserable, forcing us from our dwellings and dragging us into captivity and hard labor. Finally, those who could, fled as far away as possible in order to escape the merciless rule of the humans.

"But even there these humans pursued us. There is no end to their violence! They beat us, whip us, slaughter us, flay and chop us up. They pluck our feathers, and they shear our hair and wool. Then, after this, they boil us in pots or roast us on spits. Now I do not see any proof in this that they are our superiors; only that might makes right. Let our Lord and King judge between us. Justice is on our side."

The King again turned to Zadone, the human representative: "What do you have to say about the violence and the injustices which the animals say you have perpetrated against them?"

Zadone replied, "We say that they are our slaves and we shall seize those whom we wish and treat them just as we would treat any other possession. Those who submit to us accept the notion that the Creator set us to rule over them—but those who break our yoke and flee—they are rebelling against God's word. The choice and the consequences are theirs."

The King asked: "But what real proof do you have that the Creator intended you to rule in this cruel way over all other living creatures?"

Ga'avah strode to the front once again and proudly answered: "Consider the beauty of our form—how our bodies stand upright, how fine our senses are, and how high is our level of knowledge. Consider also the purity of our being—we alone have souls, consciences and understanding. All these are found in us, but not in them. This proves the fact that our Creator intended us to be their masters and they to serve us as we demand."

The King turned to his Court, "These humans do have beautiful forms. Their upright bodies do seem to testify to a royal design. The animals, on the other hand, whose spines are horizontal and who walk on all fours, do appear to bear the submissive form of slaves."

III

No sooner had the King uttered these words then Mule bent his head low in shame. He hesitated in his embarrassment, then replied: "O noble and upright King, may God direct you in what is proper and keep you far from error and ignorance. Please incline your ear and listen to what I say.

The Creator did not create humanity in an upright form as proof that they are lords. Nor did the Creator make our bodies bent over as a sign that we are slaves. Rather, the Creator did this in wonderful wisdom, making each body in a form most suitable to its environment.

When God created the first humans, they were naked and bare, without feathers or wool on their bodies to protect them against heat and cold. God gave them the fruit of the trees for sustenance and the humans covered their naked bodies with the leaves of the

16

trees. And since trees stand tall, the Creator accordingly made people upright in order to make it easier for them to pick fruit to eat and leaves with which to clothe themselves.

Similarly, because God gave the grass of the earth and the greenery of the field to us as food, the Creator made us walk on all fours in order for us to graze more easily on the land. Put otherwise, if we were upright, it would be difficult for us to bend over all the time to eat. If height demonstrates lordliness and lowliness servitude, then wouldn't the trees be everyone's master and all of us their servants? It is utter nonsense!"

But Ga'avah retorted: "How can you say that you have perfectly proportioned forms? Look: the camel has a big body, a long neck, small ears and a short tail. Or consider the elephant, with its long trunk and large ears but small eyes. Or cattle—long tails and horns, but no upper teeth. On the one hand, sheep have big horns and a fat tail, but no beard; while, on the other hand, the goat has a long beard, but no fat tail to cover its nakedness. Or look at the rabbit: a little body with big ears. And so it is with the majority of animals and birds and creeping, crawling things—they all lack proportion!"

"You call yourself a sage," interrupted Mule, "yet you don't even understand the basics! You are ignorant, and furthermore you have no manners. Don't you know the saying: 'One who puts another to shame is himself shamed.' You deny that we are all equally works of the Creator. God formed us all as we are for a specific reason and made each of us in a particular shape to give each species a specific advantage. No one can calculate all these except the One who created us all. You do not have the Creator's vision."

Zadone sneered at the mule: "I didn't claim to have the Creator's vision. But tell me. How does a long neck benefit a camel?"

Mule smiled: "Notice that the length of its neck corresponds to the length of its body, so that it can pick up grass from the earth yet maintain its balance. It also enables the camel to extend its mouth to every place on its body in order to scratch itself. Similarly, the trunk of the elephant compensates for the shortness of its neck. And its ears drive away flies and gnats from its eyes and especially from its mouth, which is always open because of the tusks. And the tusks were made to serve as weapons. Then again, to compensate for its being thin skinned and tiny, the ears of the rabbit are large so that it can hear the slightest sounds around it, and thus its hearing provides an extra sensitivity to and awareness of its environment beyond all of ours. And so it is with every living creature. God made us all with the limbs and parts that are most beneficial to us and that keep us safe from harm."

Cow horned in: "The fact that you, human, think you have a more beautiful form than us is no proof that you are lords over us or that we are your slaves. Our males and our females are as pleasant in each other's eyes as yours are to each other, and they are attracted to each other just as yours are. So you cannot glorify yourself over us as being more beautiful in form. Beauty of form is in the eye of the beholder."

As soon as she finished speaking, Ox added: "The gifts of the Creator are many and precious. One cannot find them all in any one creature. Rather, they are spread among all living creatures. Some may appear to have more advantages, some less, but none is perfect. The only complete and perfectly whole being is the Creator. So, in truth, we all are divinely made but, although you humans are given very honorable gifts as your portion, you are not content and must exalt yourselves over other living creatures, diminishing us and exploiting us whenever you can. What does this say about you?"

IV

When Bersaf the King heard these words, he turned to the people and said: "The arguments made by the beasts are convincing. Can you refute their claims? If so, speak."

Zadone replied: "Yes, my lord. Let me begin by saying that it grieves me to hear such anger and resentment from these animals. Why, we love and cherish these creatures because they are our dearest possessions. We raise them, house them and feed them. We protect them from strangers, bad weather and animals of prey. We heal them when they're sick. We incur many expenses to help them when they are injured. Some we honor with ornaments, like horses, which we adorn with finery and embroidered dress. All this shows our love and graciousness toward them. We do all this because they represent the proper way for lords to treat their slaves. We never abuse these animals; they abuse us by being ungrateful for the love we give them."

Mule was dumbfounded at the arrogance and duplicity of the human's words. He didn't know what to say. His heart thumped in his throat, calling him to speak, and he blurted out with pleading eyes: "Do not believe him!...He lies! Do not believe him!" Surprised at his own audacity, Mule lowered his head and, with more humility (as befitting when addressing a judge or king) spoke clearly, "My Lord..."

The King scowled at Mule: "What did you say? Have you a proper response?"

Thinking quickly, Mule added: "I am sorry to cry out. Please forgive me. But this person lies, which makes the pains they inflict upon us hurt even more. Do not believe what this man said about feeding, watering and sheltering us out of loving compassion. God forbid! It is not so! Oh...I am sorry to yell, please just try to understand our situation. Humans do these good things only because they fear that our worth will diminish. They do these things only in order to gain great benefit from us—drinking our milk, shearing our wool, riding on our backs, putting loads on us, stripping our skins for leather, and eating the flesh of our young. In the end of the matter, a cup of cruelty has been given us to drink. They certainly do not act from compassion and mercy as this human has argued."

At this, Mule was unable to restrain himself from weeping, and he cried loud and long until he could not utter another sound. His heart sank to the pit of his belly, and his mind was lost in a whirlwind of grief that, it seemed to him, none felt but he. However,

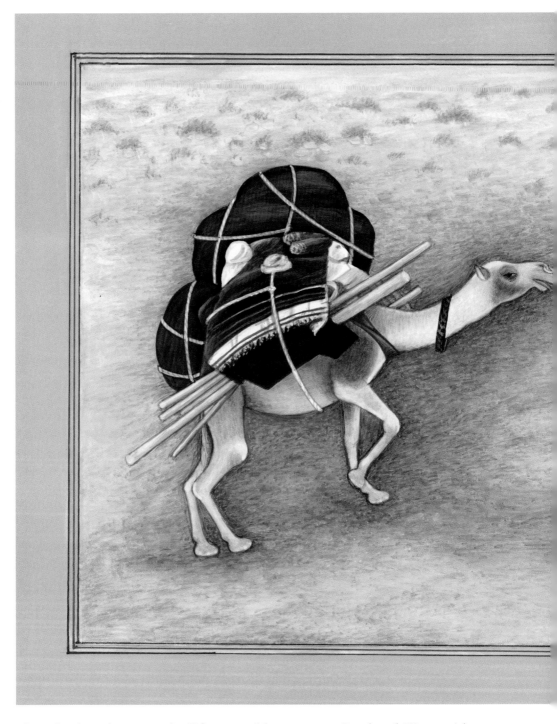

Camel spit and sputtered: "If you could see us, our Lord and King, with our nostrils pierced through with rings of iron and how they pull us by these rings causing us great pain. If you could see how they lead us in darkness through dry and desolate lands, and how we return lame,

our backs raw and aching from the friction of the heavy loads, faint with hunger, at the end of our strength—why you would cry out: 'Where is this compassion which these humans claim to have?!' Look upon us, our lord and King, and judge!"

many of his sisters and brothers cried with him, for they also knew all too well of the pain he communicated. And this eased his suffering a bit.

"Brother," brayed Donkey, "Let me take over now, you spoke your piece well, my friend. My Lord and King, it is true that, like slaves, we are acquired by them and sold by them. But so too are the Persians by the Romans and the Romans by the Persians; and the Ethiopians by the Turks and the Turks by the Ethiopians. How many peoples have taken slaves of another? And how many peoples have been taken as slaves? How can anyone prove which of them truly are lords and which are slaves? At any one time, this one governs the other, and at another time it is reversed—it is just a matter of power. So it is with us. Today we may be ruled by humankind, but God alone knows what tomorrow may bring. Perhaps someday they shall be ruled by us.

Alas, righteous King, if only you could see how we are fettered by human hands, and how our spines are crushed under the weight of packs, rocks and bricks, dirt and iron, and anything else that they deem necessary for their existence! They load us up with so much that we break down under our burdens. The last thing I feel before I go to sleep is the sharp pain in my back from the labor they impose upon me. But that is not all. Their young and old come after us with goads or sticks and hit us on our faces and backs. It is fun for them, and they laugh at us. We have no choice but to accept their cruelty; we are left to suffer alone with no one to understand our sorrows. If you saw these things, you would be moved to pity for us and you would cry out: 'Is there a decent human among them?! Is there any one with a clean heart?! Where is this compassion they pride themselves on?!'"

Turning to the other animals, Donkey urged their support: "Come, brothers and sisters, speak up and tell this court what the humans do to your kind."

And one by one each beast stepped forward with its own tale of woe.

Ox lumbered to the front and snorted: "If you could see us, our Lord and King, bound by rope to a yoke and between our shoulders the harness of a plough; how they compel us with whips and chains beyond the limits of our endurance to plough their land and to thresh their grain—and we with our mouths all bridled and muzzled—then your mercies would be so aroused you would exclaim: 'Human compassion is nothing but a fraud!'"

Camel spit and sputtered: "If you could see us, our Lord and King, with our nostrils pierced through with rings of iron and how they pull us by these rings causing us great pain. If you could see how they lead us in darkness through dry and desolate lands, and how we return lame, our backs raw and aching from the friction of the heavy loads, faint with hunger, at the end of our strength—why you would cry out: 'Where is this compassion which these humans claim to have?!' Look upon us, our lord and King, and judge!"

Then Elephant sadly trumpeted: "If you could see us hobbled by leg irons, with yokes of iron choking our necks, being beaten on the face and head by chains or whips or staves to steer us one way or another against our will—you would cry out with a bitter soul."

And Horse whinnied: "If you could see us forced into their battles with bridles in our mouths, girdles girding our loins, saddles on our backs and cinches around our bellies; how they dress us in coats of mail and arm us with weapons; and how they stab us with spurs and drive us on to face their enemies. If you could see how their weapons pierce us over and over again until we die or, if lucky, we limp homeward wounded and covered in blood—cry over us, our King, and pour forth your mercy on this, our sorrow! We need your help…"

Sheep jumped in, adding: "If you could see with your own eyes, our Lord and King, how they steal our infants and young, separating mother from child in order to drink our milk; and how they bind up the legs of our children and carry them away to be killed; how our young are beaten and left hungry and thirsty, crying and moaning in suffocating fear. If you could see how we are slaughtered and our skins stripped away and our bodies cut open…

Then in their markets, there are merchants selling meat cooked in pots, meat roasted on spits, meat baked in ovens or fried in pans—why that's us! It's our bodies they're cooking and selling! So where is the mercy and compassion which these humans contend they show us? Go and consider, O righteous King, what they do even now!"

Finally, Mule composed himself enough to utter his own tale of woe: "If you could see, our Lord, how the humans hit us, back and front, with sticks and hard staves, and how they insult and curse us with their foul mouths—if you consider, our Lord and King, how much they resemble in character the disgraceful ugliness of their words, then you would see how far removed these humans are from their supposed ideal."

Mule turned to the humans, feeling strength rising from his belly to fuel his words: "These humans fool even themselves!" He turned back to the King, "They do not follow God's commandments; they are not corrected by the rebukes of their prophets—they are incorrigible! Judge them. Judge them for their arrogance, for their violence, and for their cruelty! Judge them with eyes of justice."

As Mule finished speaking, all the cloven hoofed animals roared and cried out as if with one voice: "HAVE MERCY UPON US, our Lord and King! SAVE US FROM THE HAND OF THESE CRUEL AND OPPRESSIVE HUMANS!"

King Bersaf was deeply moved by their plea but, seeking confirmation of his feelings, he turned to his sages and sought their counsel.

"Our Lord and King," they each replied one after another, "Everything these beasts have said is true and there are many witnesses to their mistreatment at human hands."

Hearing this, the King grew increasingly purple with rage, but he calmed himself, regained his composure, and commanded: "Go to your dwellings and sleep, each human and animal in his or her own place. Return tomorrow before me and I will continue to hear arguments in this case."

GATE TWO

The consultations of the King with his ministers,
sages and judges; of the humans by themselves; and
of the animals by themselves

I

That night, the King arose and wandered in his garden with his teacher, Peruz, an enlightened spirit and a brilliant philosopher. The King said to him: "You've heard the entire lawsuit so far—what is your advice in this matter?"

Peruz responded: "If it pleases my Lord, my advice is for the King to command that all the judges and wise ones of the spirits be assembled in this court so that he may consult with them on this matter. This is a profound case with much dependent on its outcome. We are making a decision here, not only for our domain, but ultimately for animals and humans the world over."

The King nodded: "Your advice is good. As you have advised, so shall it be."

So the King's message was sent throughout the kingdom to bring the spirit judges, sages, logicians and philosophers from the spirit tribes of Na'ahid, Baharam, Babakan, Balakiss and Adariss to come to sit before their King. And so they did. And when all were gathered in the palace, he said to them: "You've heard, no doubt, of the animals' complaint about the violence done them by the humans. Behold—they take refuge in our shadow and trust in our government. What do you advise us to do?"

The chief sage from Na'ahid answered: "My advice is that the King command the animals to write a brief detailing their complaint against the humans and that this letter be read in court. Then the

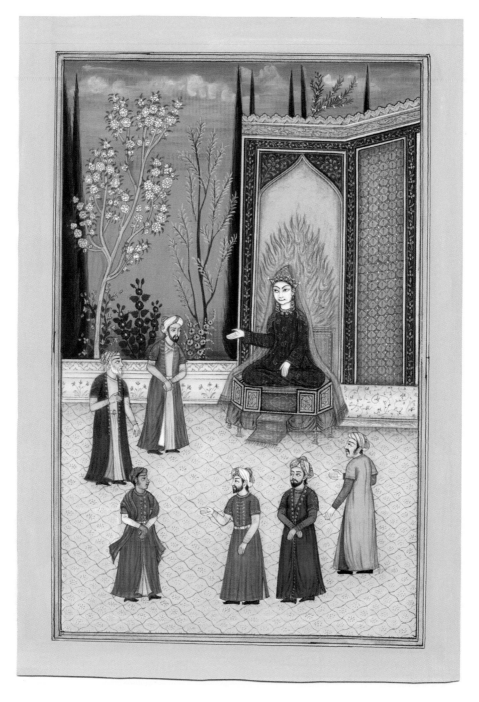

So the King's message was sent throughout the kingdom to bring the spirit judges, sages, logicians and philosophers from the spirit tribes.

judges shall judge the case to determine how the animals are to be set free. Consequently, if the humans don't do what the judges order them to do and the animals flee from them, then the humans will be the guilty ones and the animals will be absolved from any wrongdoing in fleeing."

Then the King asked the gathering: "What do you think?"

They all responded that his advice was sound; all except the sage from Baharam, who queried: "Don't you think that the humans are entitled to some compensation? Perhaps the animals should be purchased from the humans and then set free? Then the humans would be more inclined to obey the verdict."

"Yes," some answered, "that could be a good solution."

"Then who should pay the price?"

"Our Lord and King," replied the wise ones without hesitation.

So the sage asked: "Where will the King get the money?"

"From the Spirits' Treasury," they replied, again without hesitation.

The sage spoke up with a calm voice, "There isn't enough money in the House of the Spirits to pay the price of all these animals. And most humans would not want to sell the animals at any price—they use the animals to help them, they depend upon the animals for their current way of life. Kings and princes ride them and farmers use them for work in the field. They need them for food and clothing. Their minds will not change on this matter because money is not the object. There is no possibility that the animals' freedom can simply be purchased."

The King asked: "So what is your best advice?"

He replied: "I think that the King should command the captive animals to agree in secret to flee, altogether on one night, and get out from under human thumbs just as the animals of the wilderness have done. Then, when the humans awake in the morning, they won't find any creature on which to ride or with which to carry their loads. This will be the salvation of the animals from the yoke of the humans! Maybe then they will understand how much they need the animals. Maybe then they will treat them with respect."

But the leader of the sages from Babakan sourly countered: "In my opinion, this idea won't work. It will be most difficult to carry out because these animals are restrained with ropes and iron chains on their legs and shoulders at night. So how will all be able to flee during the night?"

The Master of Oaths and Incantations responded: "Let the King send bands of spirits to open the animals' bonds and loosen their bindings and transport them far away from the humans."

Turning to the King, he added: "Know, my master, that this deed would gain us great merit in the eyes of the animals and before God, as we are taught: 'Know, you King, that you are not set to rule in order to acquire wealth by collecting silver and gold, but to pay attention to the cry of the oppressed.' You have a moral obligation here, your Highness."

But the philosopher from Adariss rejected this, saying: "This flowery deed will not guarantee the outcome we desire nor will it fix what is broken. Don't you see what will happen if we deliver these animals from human bondage? Won't the humans wake up the next morning and realize that the flight of the animals altogether in one night was the work of the spirits? And when they realize that the spirits are the cause of this situation, don't you think that a hot anger will arise in their hearts and a great hatred will develop among the humans against us spirits?"

And the assembly agreed in collective recognition.

The philosopher continued, his vision seeing deep and clear: "My Lord, the King... My advice is not to pass judgment except after a complete and proper investigation of the entire matter. The King should sit in the Place of Judgment tomorrow, and the participants in the lawsuit should come before him, and the King should listen to all the arguments until it becomes clear where justice resides and then he should judge between the two parties, carefully considering all the consequences of his decision."

The philosopher then looked deeply into the King's bright eyes, and saw radiating in them a noble heart. His face warmed in admiration and he said. "A wise spirit is aware of all the possible paths and strives to choose the one that is most in accordance with God's Will. This should become clearer to us with our work and patience and, with God's Grace, we will render a just and right verdict."

But the Master of Oaths and Incantations interrupted him and, after respectfully acknowledging this truth, he asked some sober and deeply concerned questions: "Have you ever seen animals get the better of humans in a dispute? Don't humans have the advantage in speaking and presenting their views? Just look at the poor animals—should they bear this yoke forever?"

The discussion went on all night, but in the end, all agreed that the philosopher from Adariss had suggested the best path to follow.

II

While the King was occupied with his sages, the humans also gathered in a secret assembly.

Ka'as opened the meeting: "We all saw what happened today! Do any of you have any doubt about the King's inclination in this matter or how he will judge us? I'll tell you what I think. I think we've got a serious problem on our hands, and words won't solve it! Words are empty, action is what speaks!"

Ahzar and Unf shouted: "Hear, Hear!"

The wise woman, Hochmah spoke up, gently but firmly: "I think that this case can only result in one of three verdicts. One, they might rule to set the animals free from our enslavement without compensation to us. Two, we may be forced to sell them for some price. Or three, we may have to ease their yokes and improve their lot. These are the only alternatives."

Some laughed and some snickered. But Zadone sneered: "And do you know which of the three the King will choose?"

Hochmah responded mildly: "If you truly want my opinion, I will not lie to you. I think that the King will reason: 'The animals came to our court to hide under our wing; they trusted in our rule yet even here they were oppressed. Therefore we must save them from the violence done to them.' That's what he will think. So, friends, I am certain that we cannot win this case based on keeping things as they are. We should think creatively and plan for alternatives."

Concerned, one person blurted out: "But if the King judges that the beasts should be set free, what will we do? How will we survive?" The room erupted in conversation, voices rising in the crowd.

"We'll die."

"We don't need them!"

"It is our right!"

"What about our needs?"

Unf jumped up, looking at Hochmah with contempt, and then spoke above the crowd: "We must hold to our original story: 'They are our slaves and our possessions for all eternity; they are our inheritance from our parents and our ancestors, by divine right. We cannot just let them go. It wouldn't be right. Why, we'd be rewarding rebellion!'"

"We can't let that happen!" added Zadone, "We must keep our way of life. If we're asked for proof of ownership, we can simply say that the documents were lost in the Flood during Noah's time. They'll have to believe us."

But another person worried: "But if the King decides that we should sell them, what will we do?"

A city-dweller responded: "Well then, we shall sell them at a good rate and make a decent profit from them."

But a country-dweller exclaimed: "We'll all die if we are forced to free the animals, so don't even think about doing this!"

The city-dwellers were perplexed and astonished by this response and asked why. The peasant answered: "Without milk to drink and meat to eat, without wool clothes or skins to cover us, without hides to make tents, without shoes and sandals on our feet, and without skins in which to put water—why we would be naked and bare, hungry and thirsty! Indeed, death would be better than life in this case!

And don't think it is only our problem. What happens to us will ultimately happen to you city folk. Just remember where all your foods and fineries come from. So—we mustn't sell them or send them away—let's not even talk about this anymore! Instead let's improve things and make the world a little easier for them—just as Hochmah said. We should lessen the animals' toil and not work them so hard, for they are flesh and blood like us—they feel pain as we do. In this way, we will avert God's punishment, for the Creator gave them into our hands and we don't want to be found sinning. We're only hurting ourselves."

Hochmah nodded her approval as the man spoke and many other people also murmured their agreement. Ka'as glared at them all and Zadone walked towards the peasant until he stood right in his face. Then he sneered sarcastically: "Are you really so stupid? There must be a better alternative than this! It would be ridiculous for lords to treat slaves in such a manner! They must know their place. Don't look away from me! Look into my eyes. You see that I am right. Ha! You can't even look at me. You know I'm right."

"No. But I am beginning to think that violence is not the way of life that God intended for us, and that it will always come back to haunt us as long as we depend upon it for our survival. We can't rule with violence"

"Ha! You fool! What do you know? You're a peasant! You depend upon our power for your survival. Just listen to this man! HA!"

Ahzar, Unf, and their gang broke into harsh laughter, and others supported them by pounding their clubs, sticks and feet on the floor, dissolving the meeting with their unspoken tactics. But, even though the meeting adjourned with Zadone still in charge, a distinct division in the human tent was beginning to emerge.

III

That same evening, the animals also gathered in seclusion to take counsel together.

Horse was puzzled. "Considering all the hardships that have befallen us, how is it that the Court didn't rule immediately in our favor?"

Ox snorted: "Perhaps tomorrow we should return and utter an even greater and more bitter cry—maybe then the King will have mercy on us and cut our bonds—for it's clear that his compassion already has been aroused."

Elephant rumbled: "I worry that tomorrow one of the humans will be able to press their advantage by using eloquent words. Humans can be infinitely deceitful. We should come up with a plan so that the humans can't trick the judges. We need to show the Spirit King the full extent of the problem we animals face."

Mule agreed: "I think we ought to send emissaries to all of the other animal species on the island, and ask them to join us in this lawsuit. For it isn't against us alone that the humans do evil, but by extension against all species of creatures. We need the other species to unite with us. They can help us by sending the best representatives they have to stand with us. In this way we'll receive much good advice and be able to offer more effective arguments. Don't forget: 'As helpers multiply, success increases.' We are in this together; our voices must unite for the ears of justice to hear."

Those present were all of one mind, so they sent six emissaries to the rulers of the six classes of animals that were not already represented by the beasts with the cloven hoofs, which constitute the seventh species. The first emissary was Horse, who went to Lion, ruler of the carnivores, the predatory animals. The second was Ox, who went to Phoenix, ruler of the non-predatory birds. Next was Sheep, who went to Osprey, ruler of the birds of prey. Then came Donkey, who went to Bee, ruler of the winged swarming things. The fifth emissary was Pig, who went to Sea Dragon, ruler of the water creatures. And last was Mule, who went to Snake, ruler of the creeping things.

GATE THREE

The beasts send emissaries to the other species to ask
for help in their lawsuit against the humans

I

Horse, the first emissary, galloped for several hours until he reached
the green, grassy domain of Lion, king of the carnivorous animals.
The mighty monarch, unaware of what had transpired elsewhere
on the island, was lounging by a watering hole, surrounded by a
pack of lionesses. Sniffing the air, they all looked up with interest
as Horse appeared. He spoke from a prudent distance, relating to
all of them what had happened, then drawing closer he added:
"They have sent me to you, O king of beasts, to ask that you send an
advocate to stand with us in this lawsuit."

Lion shook his mane, scowled and growled out: "What are the humans arguing?"

"They say that we are their slaves and property; that they are masters over us and over all other species of animals on the face of the
earth."

Lion's growl turned to a roar: "And in what do the humans glorify
themselves that they consider themselves to be our masters? They
are weak, throw a human into a ring with me and see what happens. Are they greater in strength or power? No. Or in girth of
body or bulk of limbs? No. In jumping or running, or in natural
weaponry? No! Let them feel my teeth penetrate their skin as I
snack on their salty flesh. They shall watch me as I eat them alive.
Let them stand in battle with my kind and see what happens. Behold, if they glorify themselves as our masters, and demonize us as
their slaves, I will gather my forces and fall upon them suddenly.

And Lion began to slash the air with his talons and gnash his teeth in fury....Quivering from head to hoof, Horse whimpered: "By my life, your majesty, there are humans who glorify themselves in all ways above us. But they are too clever to rely solely on their own strength." When Lion heard the words of the emissary, he stood dumbstruck for a while, then he commanded that word be spread throughout his kingdom that all his forces should gather before him: all the meat-eaters with incisors and talons— tigers and wolves, polecats and jackals, bears and foxes, wildcats, hyenas, and more.

We will tear apart their ranks and teach them what power really is!" And Lion began to slash the air with his talons and gnash his teeth in fury.

Quivering from head to hoof, Horse whimpered: "By my life, your majesty, there are humans who glorify themselves in all ways above us. But they are too clever to rely solely on their own strength." The Lion king stopped his display and listened with concerned curiosity.

"They make swords and spears, knives and hooks, slings and bows. And they have unusual clothes—coats of mail and iron shoes and copper girdles. The sharp teeth of young lions won't be able to grab hold of them, nor will the teeth of a tiger be able to gash them. You carnivores don't know the depth of human cunning. But the dispute before the King and his ministers is not based on strength; rather it is based on argument and other demonstrations of wisdom."

When Lion heard the words of the emissary, he stood dumbstruck for a while, then he commanded that word be spread throughout his kingdom that all his forces should gather before him: all the meat-eaters with incisors and talons—tigers and wolves, polecats and jackals, bears and foxes, wildcats, hyenas, and more. The king made known to them the story of the emissary, adding: "Now who will be the one to go and speak in our name, to return home to great honor? Who will defend us, not with violence, but with words expressing our right to life? We will help provide him with everything he needs to say."

But all those assembled were struck silent because they feared in their hearts that there was none among them worthy of the task.

Tiger said: "My master the king, if the matter were to be decided by leaping and killing in a single bound—behold, I'd be good for that."

Wolf said: "If it depended on coming in stealth to steal sheep and cattle, then I'd be the obvious choice."

Bear said: "If the matter only had to do with making ambushes in narrow places, then I'd do it."

Lion king looked expectantly to Horse, but the horse shook his head firmly from side to side.

Cat said: "If it were a matter of pretending modesty and meekness, of lying in their midst with shut eyes and appearing to doze while my heart is alert—behold I'd be perfect."

Dog said: "If it were a matter of servile flattery, of wagging the tail and following after them expectantly, then I could certainly do the job."

But the king said sadly: "You are all fine warriors. I'm sorry, but I can't pick any of you because the problem requires other skills. We need someone who is wise and articulate, not just strong." The king began to roar in despair.

After some thought, Tiger spoke up: "Sire, I think that there is none as understanding and wise and good as Dragon.

All those assembled howled and roared their agreement, so Lion called for Dragon and said: "For the honor of our species, go and represent us. Be careful with your words and return with justice served. We are depending on you in trust."

The king helped him with what to say, and sent him on his way in the company of Horse.

II

The kingdom of the non-predatory birds extended throughout the island, but its king, Phoenix, dwelt in the desert. Ox, the second emissary, lumbered along for half the night before reaching the court. By the time he arrived, word had already reached the kingdom and Phoenix had already gathered flocks of all the non-predatory birds

Ox, the second emissary, lumbered along for half the night before reaching the court. By the time he arrived, word had already reached the kingdom and Phoenix had already gathered flocks of all the non-predatory birds to his side. There they hopped and fluttered, covering the rocky desert floor in numbers so great it was impossible to count them. Ox looked upon the sea of birds, and told them about the plan....Phoenix, the king, turned to Peacock, his advisor, and asked: "Whom do we have who would be a worthy spokes-bird?"

to his side. There they hopped and fluttered, covering the rocky desert floor in numbers so great it was impossible to count them. Ox looked upon the sea of birds, and told them about the plan.

Phoenix, the king, turned to Peacock, his advisor, and asked: "Whom do we have who would be a worthy spokes-bird?"

Stretching his tail feathers in agitation, Peacock hedged: "My lord, our kinds are so numerous! I don't even know where to begin!"

Phoenix snapped: "Just begin, you peacock!"

So Peacock began strutting about, reciting: "Lapwing, the spy, is friend and beloved of Solomon the King, the son of David. He dresses in many colors and wears a mantle on his head and shakes it as if praying. It was he who first told Solomon about the Queen of Sheba. Then there's Rooster who calls to prayer. He is the one who stands on a wall with a red waddle on his head like a crown, and with red eyes. He spreads his wings and makes his tail stand up like a flag. He knows the times of prayer and awakens the humans to their duties. Now Lark is an advisor and advocate. At midday she gives advice, acting like a preacher on the pulpit.

And then there is Thrush, the imitator, who stands on a branch of a fruit tree. She is small of body, quick of movement and white of cheek, with darting eyes and a clear and pleasant voice. She dwells with humans in their orchards and mixes with them in their homes. She answers to all who call and imitates tunes and chirps. Raven, on the other hand, makes prophecies. He is the one dressed in black, zealous in his lamentations every dawn. He goes everywhere because he is strong winged. He walks down distant roads and roams the far places, tells futures, announces hidden things, and says in his cry: 'Beware! Visions! Danger, danger!...'"

"Stop!" interrupted Phoenix, "Just tell me who, in your eyes, is most worthy to represent our species in the lawsuit with the humans?"

And Peacock responded: "All are proper and right for this, because all are fluent, poetic and masters of language, but Nightingale is a master both of tongues and tunes—she is the one who stands on the branch of a tree, tiny of body, easy of movement and good of song. Send Nightingale, for there is none like her in your domain."

And the Phoenix turned to Nightingale and said, "Go and speak as boldly as inspiration speaks to you!" And she flew off as commanded, leaving Ox to lumber after her as fast as he could.

III

Meanwhile, the third emissary, Sheep, was sent to the seashore, to meet Osprey, queen of the birds of prey, dwelling high atop a rocky, wind-lashed promontory. Osprey is a bird so great in size that she could have grasped the sheep in one talon and easily lifted both herself and her prey skyward. And she and the sheep both knew it. Nonetheless, Sheep summoned up all her courage to stand before her. The queen listened to the sheep with a pensive scowl. And with a strong call, all the birds of prey appeared in seconds in response to their queen's command. The air was filled with all sorts of predatory birds: eagles and vultures, owls and bustards, falcons and hawks and buzzards, and more besides.

Then Queen Osprey told them all that the emissary had told her, adding: "You have heard, families of hunting birds, about the trouble which the humans have brought upon us in their self-aggrandizement over all other living creatures! Until this matter came up we have managed to keep ourselves far removed from them, seeking peace and security far from their evil. And yet despite all this, it has not saved us because now we must go to court to defend our rights. But do not despair—God pays all according to their deeds."

The queen continued: "To think how I've helped those uncaring creatures over the years! How many ships have I saved by sending them in the right direction! How many boats sank while I helped the survivors reach dry land! Why do I do these things? I'll tell you

How many boats sank while I helped the survivors reach dry land! Why do I do these things? I'll tell you why — I do them as a way of honoring God for having given me such a great and strong body!" The queen broke off her brooding in agitation.

why—I do them as a way of honoring the Creator for having given me such a great and strong body!" The queen broke off her brooding in agitation.

Turning to Falcon, her advisor, she asked: "Who should go to the King of the spirits?"

The advisor said: "I see no one better for this than Owl because our other hunters avoid humans and don't understand their words. But Owl dwells near them and is modest and humble and doesn't covet."

But Owl replied: "This is true, but I shouldn't go because the humans think I am a sorcerer's accomplice, and despise and curse me though I do them no wrong."

"Who would be better?" asked the queen.

"Behold, humans love birds of prey like Hawk." replied Owl. "They use them to hunt. Perhaps your Highness should send one of their kind."

But Hawk countered: "Unfortunately, the humans do not respect us for our ideas, but rather because we provide a means of livelihood. They send us out to hunt, then take away our prey, and so collect from us that which we get by the sweat of our brow. And this leads them to the sins of laziness and gluttony."

Osprey the queen grew impatient: "So whom do you think we should send?"

"My queen," said Falcon, her advisor, "Perhaps Parrot would go. Humans love his kind. Their kings and nobles raise them in their palaces and gain status from having them. They speak to Parrot and he imitates their words and sayings, repeating back to them what he has just heard. Parrot—am I right?"

"Right!" repeated Parrot. Then he added: "My queen, I will go, and, with the help of God, argue with the humans for our good."

So they blessed Parrot and sent him on his way with Sheep.

IV

The fourth emissary, Donkey, meanwhile had trotted as fast as he could, first through the meadowlands and then into the green forest, searching for the home of Bee, the queen of the swarming flying things. And there, among the branches of a mighty banyan tree, Donkey saw Bee's nest. The Queen, of course, already knew what had transpired—for word travels swiftly among the wee winged ones. She had already gathered to her side every kind of swarming flying thing: bees and wasps, flies and mosquitoes, butterflies and gnats, fleas and bugs, and grasshoppers and locusts— and all the other creatures with small bodies which fly with wings, but don't have feathers or fur or hair, and which don't live even a full year. They were so many that the sky was dark with their numbers. Then Bee told them of the beasts' case before King Bersaf and asked for a volunteer.

The leader of the wasps said: "I will go to represent the community!"

But the lord of the flies opposed this, asserting: "No, we will go!"

"No, we will go!" the leader of the locusts chirped.

"Each of you is yearning to go," the Bee wondered. "Why do you think you can succeed against the humans? After all, they are so huge compared to our kind."

Wasp snickered: "Even though a man arms himself with weapons, if one of us comes along and bites him with a sting no worse than the prick of a needle, he gets so worried and alarmed that he drops everything; his skin bubbles up in a bump and it hurts him to the point that he is unable to wear or carry his weapons."

And Fly replied: "Even the most honored and awesome among them has to use the toilet, and when he does, then we fly about his clothes and face to bite him and he is not able to chase us away!"

And Flea said with glee: "Is it not so that when one of us comes between a person and his clothes and gives him just a little bite, we disturb him so much that he wants to grab us in his hand, but we always manage to jump free."

The queen laughed and said: "You are all right, size does not make any difference! But at the Court of the King of the spirits, ideas and clear thinking will be what count—do any of you have these skills?"

The assembly stood dumbfounded, thinking silently about what the queen had said. Then the wisest of the bee sages said: "Behold, it is apparent that only you, our queen, with the help of the Creator, can fulfill this task."

So off she flew in the company of Donkey to the Court of the Spirit King.

V

Pig, the fifth emissary, traveled long and far to arrive at the lair of Sea Dragon, ruler of all the water creatures. By the time she arrived at Sea Dragon's huge cavern by the shore of the Green Sea, the king had already gathered everyone to his court: crocodiles, serpents, dolphins, crabs, shelled creatures, turtles, fish and frogs from the seas, rivers, lakes, and ponds—altogether some seven thousand different kinds—and told them of the case of the four-legged creatures.

Inhaling breath upon breath, Sea Dragon exclaimed: "In what do these humans glorify themselves? If it is in size of body or strength— I will go there and with one fiery breath I will burn them up; and after that I will inhale and swallow them all as a snack!"

"Your majesty," Pig demurred gently, "Humans don't pride themselves in these matters, but in clever reasoning and subtlety."

"But why not destroy them if they threaten us?"

"Then we would be no better than them. Our fear may fuel our aggressive instincts, which would lead us to war, but one war begets another, and the violence would never end. If we wish to lead a

Sea Dragon exclained, "I will go there and with one fiery breath I will burn them up, and after that I will inhale and swallow them all as a snack!"

peaceful life, we must find a way to co-exist together. It is my hope that one day the humans will know the value of life, and will be able to see past their own greed. And if we fight them with force, we will most likely lose. They use their intelligence to create weapons to destroy and control life. No doubt if we fight them, we will all die."

"Do you doubt my strength?"

"Oh, no your majesty! But please don't let your pride blind you..."

And Sea Dragon shut his eyes and took a huge, deep breath, first to calm himself and then to examine his motivations. Opening his eyes again, he responded with renewed humility, "These humans sound dangerous. Perhaps you'd better tell me a little more. Tell me what you see, tell me about them so that I may know what they are."

"As my lord and king commands", Pig replied. "Humans can descend into the depths of the sea and bring forth pearls, crystal and coral. They know how to make traps to bring eagles down from the high mountains. They make wagons from trees and fasten oxen, buffalo and horses to them forcing them to haul heavy loads from dawn to dusk. They make their way into the wilderness and lay paths of stone. They build ships that rove from one end of the earth to the other. They dig holes and enter into caves and caverns to extract minerals, metals and precious stones. In short, they can do everything but fly or breathe underwater! They are clever, and there seems to be no limit to the violence of which they are capable."

When Sea Dragon heard the words of Pig, he was aghast. Finally, he turned to those around him and asked: "What is your advice? Who shall go on our behalf?"

And they said: "Let Whale go because she is a hunter and the biggest creature in the sea! Furthermore, she should receive the honor because she saved a prophet, Jonah, and guarded him in her belly three days before casting him out alive and well."

But Whale objected: "My lord, I would go, but I lack legs and, not only that, but you know I cannot live even an hour outside the water. However, I think that Salamander would be right for the job because she lives in water but also goes up from the water to dwell on land. She lives on dry land just as she lives in water and she breathes in air just like she breathes in water."

But Salamander deferred to yet another: "I am not right for this mission because I am slow in walking and the road is very long. Crab would be better for this task because he has big legs, walks well and quickly, has powerful claws, and his back is hard like armor."

All heads turned to look at Crab, but Crab would have none of it: "I won't go and that's final. The way I look, I fear being mocked and disgraced. When the humans see me headless, with my eyes between my shoulders and my mouth in my chest, and walking sidewards on my eight bent legs—they will explode in laughter at me!"

"I see your point," Sea Dragon said, suppressing a smile, "So whom do you think should be sent?"

"Crocodile would be a good choice because he has fast legs, a mouth full of terrible teeth, is strong-bodied and fearsome in appearance."

But Crocodile said: "I am not right because I am quick tempered and furthermore I detest all creatures except myself. Leave me be, Sire."

Pig grunted a reminder: "Remember the idea isn't to find someone with brute strength alone—no offense intended. Prudence, knowledge and understanding are what are called for."

Crocodile cast Pig a sidelong glance, stared hard for a while; then spoke to the king: "I think that Frog would make an excellent choice because she is wise and patient. Furthermore, Frog is respected by the humans on account of the good deed she did in the days of Moses when her kind helped free the slaves. Frog is one of those creatures that can live both in water and on dry land. She walks well. She is pleasant-tongued. Her head is round and her eyes sparkle. She goes hopping into the homes of humans. She doesn't fear them and they don't fear her."

Frog agreed to undertake the mission, so they gave her provisions, set her on Pig's back—for time was of the essence—and sent them speedily on their way.

VI

By the time the sixth and last emissary, Mule, found the den of Snake, monarch of all the creeping crawling things, the whole kingdom was abuzz with the news. Mule had to step carefully as he made his way to the king's rock throne because the ground was covered with creatures in numbers so great that God alone (who created them all and gives them their portions to eat) knows how many they are: vipers, snakes and scorpions, spiders and crickets, and all kinds of crawlers that swarm on stinking garbage, on land or in mud, in dirt or in caves.

Mule was astounded.

King Snake hissed to his advisor, Viper: "Whom shall we send to court, to argue on our behalf? The majority of these are deaf, dumb and blind, soft-bodied, without legs or arms or wings. Most are naked and bare, without cunning or strength."

As the king spoke, he began to cry, and his eyes filled with tears of pity and compassion for his weak and deficient subjects. And he raised his eyes to Heaven and said this prayer: "Please, O Creator and Preserver of all creatures, have mercy on Your works! Protect and guard these, Your children!"

Now when Cricket heard this, he went up on the wall and creaked his wings together, making pleasant melodies of praise to the Creator in accompaniment to his king. Then Cricket chirped: "Hear me, my lord. Don't be overly troubled by what you see in your subjects, because God's wisdom and loving-kindness sustains us all.

Know that the Creator made some creatures with big bodies and strong builds, and others with small bodies and soft builds. But each has certain unique qualities that balance or cancel the qualities of others and protect them from harm. An example of this: God gave Elephant a great body and a strong build. He deflects all harm with his long hard tusks and uses his trunk with great dexterity. God gave Gnat a tiny, weak body, it is true, but also the ability of fast flight to save it from harm. Both manifest the Creator's wisdom and each works well in its own way.

Furthermore, our kind has an easier time finding sustenance than those bigger and stronger than us. God put us everywhere—in holes, crevices, or on the bodies of animals—and we live off our surroundings. Our strength and our bodies are just the right size for what we need in order to survive. Not only that—diseases don't touch us as they do the other creatures. Praise be to the Creator who made our situations as they are!"

As Cricket concluded, King Snake declared: "How beautiful are your words and how fine your speech! Praised be the One who placed in our midst a speaker as articulate and wise as you. Go therefore and represent our species in this dispute with the humans."

"I will go to do the bidding of my king," Cricket responded, and off he went leaping in the hoofprints left by Mule who, in eagerness to be on the way, was already making tracks.

"Wait for me, brother mule," chirruped the cricket, "I need you to carry me!"

VII

And so, from every horizon and from every corner of the Island of Tsagone, the living creatures converged on the Court of Bersaf the Wise, King of the Spirits, there to stand together with the cloven-hooved beasts in their lawsuit against the humans, each living creature feeling itself as part of the family of life as never before. The six spokes-creatures— Dragon, representing the carnivorous animals; Nightingale, representing the non-predatory birds; Parrot, representing the birds of prey; Queen Bee, representing the swarming flying things; Frog, representing the water creatures; Cricket, representing the creeping crawling things—all ventured off in unified heart, bonded in their purpose to communicate their right to a life free from violence and abuse. As for the emissaries—they were utterly exhausted and went to bed—for they had traveled to the ends of the island and back, all in one short night.

GATE FOUR

The dispute between the animals and the humans at
King Bersaf's Court, and the arguments made there
by both parties

I

Later that day, everyone—all the animals, all the humans, and all
the spirits—gathered in the Court of King Bersaf. When the King
looked around and saw all the animals with their different shapes
and voices and tunes he was at once struck dumb with fascination.
After marveling at them for a long time, he turned to observe the
humans standing together, seventy in number, representing every
race, religion and nation, each dressed according to the custom of
his or her land.

After gazing at this assembly for some time, the King turned to the
spirit sages and philosophers and exclaimed: "Do you see these
awesome forms and shapes? How wondrous is their diversity! I
am astounded by the wisdom of the Creator, the One who established their forms and who differentiated their shapes, the One who
preserves and sustains us all."

Then looking around and, raising his eyes, Bersaf saw a frog sitting
on a tree by the seashore. "Who are you?" he inquired.

"I am Frog," she croaked sweetly, "emissary of the water creatures,
sent by our king, Sea Dragon, who dwells in the ocean, where the
waves begin and the thick clouds are born, the ruler of all who dwell
in water, whether salt or sweet, running or stagnant."

"And what does your king say about this matter?"

Frog replied: "My Lord and King, when Sea Dragon, our king, heard
the words of the humans and their argument against the other living creatures, he was astounded at their insolence and said:

"I am Frog," she croaked sweetly, "emissary of the water creatures, sent by our king, Sea Dragon, who dwells in the ocean, where the waves begin and the thick clouds are born, the ruler of all who dwell in water, whether salt or sweet, running or stagnant."…Frog explained: "The humans claim to be superior to us, but is there really any distinction between us and them? Just like us, sometimes they eat and sometimes they are eaten.

'What fools these humans are and how they err. How can they think that carnivores and birds of prey—not to mention snakes and crocodiles, dolphins and other big fish—are their slaves or that we were created for their sake!? Don't they realize that if we wild ones all chose to attack them, that they would be annihilated in no time at all?!'"

Frog explained: "The humans claim to be superior to us, but is there really any distinction between us and them? Just like us, sometimes they eat and sometimes they are eaten. The fact that they have dominated some cows, sheep, and horses has distorted their sense of reality. Their pride has blinded them to who they are. These creatures have neither claws nor sharp teeth with which to attack their enemies. The humans should thank God their Creator for not setting the other living creatures over them. With our numbers and combined strength, we could dominate them! So what brings them to the foolish notion that they are entitled to rule over us?"

II

When Frog finished speaking, the King looked at the assembly of humans and asked: "Tell me, humans, who is your king?"

"Our Lord," was the reply, "We have many kings."

Bersaf wondered why the human species had many kings while each animal species had but one.

One of the humans answered: "My Lord and King, the reason lies in the great diversity of people. In all the world there are seven continents, and in every continent there are many states, and in every state there are many cities, each with its own tongue and styles and ideas. For this reason people have kings in every region and district, each ruling a small portion of the world. It is impossible that all should be guided by but one king.

Furthermore, the animals' so-called kings only rule by virtue of power, not wisdom. They do not direct or order the lives of their subjects. They do not have governments. But the human species does! And this is a further proof that we are lords and they are meant to be slaves."

Parrot clacked his beak sharply: "The humans boast of their superiority, but hear it from me, o humans: For every point of pride there is a corresponding degradation. For all your good rulers there are many more oppressive ones; for all your righteous judges there are corrupt ones; for all your police there are thieves and brigands, murderers and robbers. But we are protected from all these, thank God!

The claim that your rulers are unique and different from ours is just plain rubbish. Consider the Bee: The community of bees gathers together to proclaim one queen over them. After this, the queen takes for herself workers, soldiers and companions. She pays attention to their lives and well-being, and they build wonderful homes and rooms with a gatekeeper and guards and ministers of the storehouse. Some bees become nurses, others soldiers; some are builders, others gatherers of food. And they do this freely and willingly, in a joyous and diligent manner. They enjoy their work, and let their work strengthen the noble qualities within them. They don't let their work corrupt them.

In contrast to this, most human rulers don't care a whit for the matters of their masses, except for the benefit they may derive from them. Their subjects are compelled to work for the crown and to pay taxes for its upkeep. But a good ruler should treat his subjects with mercy and act with loving-kindness towards them just as God supervises all of Creation. The rulers of all the animal species follow the Will of God, but human sovereigns do not necessarily do so."

Bersaf the King was intrigued by what Parrot had said about the bees, so he asked: "Who here represents the winged swarming things?" And suddenly the King heard a ringing, singing voice and behold here was Queen Bee hovering in the air, moving her wings with an invisible, but audible movement.

"I do! I am Queen and emissary of the bees and other winged swarming things," she buzzed.

"Why did you come by yourself and not send a representative as did the other creatures' rulers?"

"My Lord," she replied, "I felt that I alone should take the risk because of the great distance involved."

Bersaf said admiringly: "How considerate you are—just as Parrot said—please tell me more about your kind."

"Know that God has singled us out and made known to us the importance of work, the building of hives, and the establishment of storehouses in them. And the Creator has given us a unique gift, for we can produce from our bodies a sweet liquid, pleasant to eat, very healthy, and healing to the sick. The form of our bodies, with their wondrous structure, and our marvelous wings, are two more of God's gifts to us."

The King inquired how the bees got along with the humans and Queen Bee replied: "We try to build our nests far away from them and that saves most of us, but sometimes they search us out and, if they're successful, they destroy our houses and drive out our young in order to rob our storehouses and eat our provisions. Although we sometimes bear a grudge and get angry, we generally have great patience. But when we get angry and fly far away, then the humans come after us to entice us with sweet flowers so that we return to live among them. And they excuse all the cruelty they do because they believe everything is for their benefit alone; because they are our masters and we their slaves. They often can't see beyond their own appetites, beyond their own greed, and the whole world suffers for it."

The human assembly grew upset at the length of the conversation between the King and the Queen Bee. Hasad grew jealous and demanded an explanation of the spirit sages: "Why does he treat her as if she were his equal!?"

Peruz, the King's teacher and confidante, answered Hasad: "Don't be astonished by this, for the Bee is clearly virtuous and fine of soul. Furthermore, she is spokes-insect and queen of all the winged swarming things. And sovereigns always speak with their counterparts, regardless of their shape or size."

III

When Bersaf had finished speaking with Queen Bee, he turned again to the human assembly and demanded: "We've heard the complaints lodged by these animals and their cry against your oppression. And we have heard your arguments in defense. But the animals' words repudiate and contradict all your arguments. Do you have yet another point to offer in support of your claim?"

Ga'avah stood up in response, the arrogance in her voice grew as she spoke: "Our claim is best supported by our many kinds of wonderful knowledge, our great wisdom and the wondrous works of our hands. In every land, we have merchants and laborers and workers of the land; poets, linguists, philosophers, judges, lawyers; scientists and theologians; astrologers and doctors; sorcerers and alchemists; masters of talismans and astronomers; musicians and artists and all sorts of craftspeople—to mention but a few...Only we humans, I'm proud to say, have these disciplines, skills and crafts, which certainly proves what we've said, namely that we are their superiors and they therefore must be our slaves. There is a hierarchy of life, and we are at the top." She then cast an arrogant eye over the assembled creatures and smiled mockingly.

"What have you to say to this woman?" The King asked the animals. "What proof can you bring against her argument? It is a strong point, is it not?"

And the creatures stood dumbfounded, silent for a long time, thinking about the weighty advantages that the Creator had given humans—more to them than to the other living creatures.

But then Nightingale flew forward and sang out: "These humans think that their wisdom and knowledge demonstrate that they are masters and we are slaves. Not so! If they had listened to what Queen Bee said, they would know that we too have wisdom and many crafts.

Consider the ant—if these humans knew anything at all about ants— how they tunnel under the ground to make homes with rooms and attics, divided by paths and labyrinths; how they place their homes low, like drainage pipes, in order to collect water from the dew yet store their food in the upper chambers to keep it dry for sustenance during autumn; how they cut the wheat kernel in two, and how they peel the barley and bean and lentil because they know that they will not sprout afterwards; how they work zealously in summer, in heat of night and day, to prepare their homes and to collect food for their survival; how they conceal their storehouses; and how they patrol their territory every day. Consider that when one of them finds something and is not able to carry it because of its weight, her companions willingly help with a sense of urgency. Furthermore, consider also how each of them knows to follow the same path from which the first came. Consider all these, O King, and recognize that even ants have wisdom and skills and crafts just as the humans have.

The bee is more expert in building dwellings than any craftsman among you humans. She builds her home from half-circles and makes her rooms with six equal sides; moreover, she does all this without tools—unlike you humans. The silkworm quickly spins a shelter for itself without study and without tools for building, weaving or sewing. The spider weaves a web more expertly than any human weaver, tightening each thread as if it were a string of a violin or tent, yet the spider does this without tools and without materials, unlike human weavers who must use our wool or silk as raw materials, and then fashion cloth by using many tools and utensils."

Parrot interjected: "And just as these creatures have an innate ability to build, so too all of us are born knowing how to live and survive. By the Creator's design, we are born complete: with protective layers as clothing, with the ability to move around, to find food, and to get along with one another.

By contrast, consider how little knowledge your young have and how foolish they are at birth: They know nothing and have no discernment. It is only after four years—and some say seven, thirteen or even twenty years—that they gain understanding. Every day they need guidance and correction in order to survive. But our young: they are learned and understand all that is necessary for them to survive from the moment they emerge from the womb or hatch from the egg. By comparing your young and ours, it appears that Providence has blessed us over you.

And, speaking of offspring, let me tell you that we creatures raise our young more effectively. We seek neither reward nor honor from our children, but the majority of humans bind their children to them, hoping to reap reward and recompense and honor from them. Because we raise our young the way we do, God never had to command us: "Honor your father and mother." That happens naturally. All this demonstrates how truly free we are and how bound in servitude you humans are. You're not as free as you think you are; your cleverness and pride blind you to the truth. Don't you see what you are doing to us and to yourselves?"

Nightingale chimed in: "The end of the matter is this: Even the swarming and creeping creatures have knowledge and understanding and unique skills. We all do. Therefore, since we all have a portion of the Creator's gifts, how can humans glorify themselves over us and claim that they are our lords and masters?"

Glowing orange with delight, Bersaf exclaimed: "Well said! We shall explore these points further."

Nightingale chimed in: "Therefore, since we all have a portion of the Creator's gifts, how can humans glorify themselves over us and claim that they are our lords and masters?"

IV

Provoked by the King's show of admiration, another human, a round fleshy woman named Shara, stood up and objected: "We still have additional points to prove our contention.

Consider food and drink. Our food is the best of the harvest while theirs is peels, straw, and leaves. We take the fat of fruits, their juices and oils, but they only eat grasses, unripe or rotten stuff, or chunks of uncooked flesh torn off dead or decaying bodies.

We alone have invented all kinds of delicacies with our wisdom: baked cakes, breads of all kinds, tasty cheeses, and so on. And we have many kinds of cooked dishes and sauces for meats and fishes, all done in different ways: baked and boiled, roasted and broiled, pan fried, deep fried and many other kinds. There is no limit to our creativity!"

"Furthermore," she spoke, her heart drifting to the pleasures she enjoyed most in life, "We have all kinds of drinks and wines and so many kinds of sweets. But they—they know nothing about these tasty things because their food is coarse, hard, dry, and lacking in fatty oils. Now everyone knows that the way of lords is to enjoy themselves with rich foods, while slaves eat nothing but dry morsels and a bit of water. Need I say more?"

Cricket rubbed his legs with glee when he heard this recital of human gluttony: "These humans glory in the richness of their foods, their delicacies and their drinks, but they don't realize that all these actually cause distress and toil.

Not only must they make these dishes by the sweat of their brow, but consider all the trouble they have just in acquiring the ingredients: plowing and sowing and digging, making all kinds of vessels to water the shoots and plants, and digging wells. Then they must harvest the grain, collect it, thrash and winnow it and take it to the city, there to grind it, then to knead it and bake it. And to do all this they must build tools and wagons and mills and ovens and chimneys; carry water, chop wood, pick spices and so on and so on. How many tears have been shed doing this? How much weeping?

Now consider how we live. We are free of all this because the soft, moist greens we eat come ready-made from the earth and the dew of heaven. Our food grows in such great abundance that we can eat as much as we want because it shoots forth from the earth year after year, without trouble or toil, for our food is the work of the earth itself. So—when it comes to food, we are carefree whereas for them getting food is a burden and a form of slavery in itself.

Also, when one of us has eaten his fill, he leaves the rest without the need to guard it behind a locked door. We don't fear robbers or brigands—but not so with them! For them it is the opposite. The sun goes down—they all latch and lock their doors to guard body and property, but it doesn't really help because many are killed for what's inside. Once again this demonstrates that they are bound in servitude through the very things by which they claim superiority.

Another point: You humans consider honey to be one of your best foods and medicines, but it is just bee spit! You don't make it—you steal it from the winged, swarming things!

Also: although God created us as we are from the beginning—some as plant-eaters and some as meat-eaters—you humans at first were given only plants and fruits to eat. But you turned from the Creator's way and behaved badly, so God brought the Great Flood to wash away your evil from the earth. Only after the Flood, as a concession to your vile appetites, did the Creator permit Noah and his descendants to eat animal flesh. That you have learned how to catch us, kill us, spice us and cook us is no mark of your "superiority". Rather, it is a sign that you continue to fall short of our Maker's original design. And so it has remained to this very day! We however still eat exactly what the Creator first intended for us." The Cricket concluded by cranking out a tune with his wings as if to say "top that!"

The King queried: "Now what do you humans have to say!?"

V

Ga'avah arose again and proudly made her way forward: "My Lord and King, the strongest proof I can offer for our superiority is that we share the same form while they have a multitude of forms and appearances. Just as God is one; we are one. Our unity of form is a sign of rulership and lordship."

And there was great confusion and much consternation among the animals at that moment. Paws gesticulated and feathers fluttered; grunts and roars, chirps and twitters filled the hall as they strove to decide how best to answer the words of the proud woman.

Finally, Nightingale flew forward: "My Lord and King, the woman is right in part, but only superficially. Although we animals have a multitude of forms—behold our souls are one. And these humans with their single form—behold they have many souls."

The King leaned forward with great interest: "What proof do you have that their souls are disunited?"

She said: "Our Lord and King—the multitude of their religions, not to mention that within any one religion there are many diverse sects and doctrines. All have disputed beliefs, yet each claims to be the one, true path to God! And the people of this faith hate those of that faith and they fight with one another and also amongst themselves. And this religious leader curses that one and that one seeks to kill another one. It is hard to imagine what is done by these humans in God's name! We, however, are above all this—our belief is one and our faith is one. We live to praise the Creator for sustaining our lives and providing us our food."

Then another human, Shabakah by name, lustily shouted out: "We too praise the Creator every day! God honored us alone with prophecy and visions and holy books! God gave us alone numerous laws and commandments, fasts and festivals. God gave us all these as marks of honor and glory—but you animals are lacking any of these things. This proves our claim to lordship and grandeur, while your lack is a sign of inferiority."

Mule stomped his hoof with impatience and annoyance: "If you could think clearly, then you would know that all the points which you've raised contradict your own position. You alone of all the species need these sorts of rules. Were you humans treating each other as the Creator intended; then you would not have had to be commanded: "Do not kill. Do not steal. Do not commit adultery. Love God with your entire heart. Love your neighbor as yourself". God gave the commandments to you—to you and not to us—because you humans are wicked and you follow the way of rebellion. We animals don't need prophets, laws or holy books because we are innocent of transgression and sin.

Similarly, we have no need of holy days either. In your case, God had to set *at least* certain times for your hearts to be turned from other thoughts and directed towards the Creator. In our case, every place is a house of prayer and every time an occasion for worship. All days are equal and the same to us—the entire year is a festival for us, so to speak—because every day we sing songs and praises to our Creator. So you are more inclined to be in slavery while we truly are more free."

The humans huddled together for a few minutes. Then Shabakah stood up and declared: "What you say, ass, has some truth to it, but your innocence and freedom result from an utter lack of self-consciousness."

"What do you mean?" asked Bersaf in puzzlement.

"Only we human beings have a sense of self-consciousness and the best proof of this is the fact that we humans cover our nakedness by wearing all sorts of wondrous clothes and ornaments made from all sorts of materials. This not only shows our God-given wisdom and skill, but also proves our superiority. The fact that they go naked and exposed without even a care or thought demonstrates their inferiority."

Then Dragon stood and turned to the assembly of spirit sages and judges and roared out: "Have any of you ever heard as many errors and lies as this human has uttered?!"

Turning to the human, Dragon glared and retorted: "How dare you claim superiority on this basis! The clothes by which you glorify yourselves are obtained from the very creatures you despise and from the very animals you've conquered!"

Dragon continued with grave seriousness: "What you humans find most pleasant to wear is silk and wool. But surely you know that silk comes from worm cocoons and is not the work of humans and that wool comes from sheep and camels and hares? Silk is meant to be a nest for the silk worms and their young, a shelter from the extremes of weather and a nursery for the new-borns. But then you humans come and take what is theirs by violence. And so, on account of this, you are punished with everything associated with its use: purchasing, selling, manufacturing, repairing, guarding—all of which are troubling to the heart and which lie heavy on the soul. Similarly, you take our wool and skins and hair by arrogant strength. Yet you glory in these acts of oppression and violence and are not ashamed!

If clothing were indeed your honor and glory, behold it would be more fitting for us to glorify ourselves by these things than you. Our young are born wearing what is most suitable to them: hair or wool or feathers or scales or shells. And this is clothing and decoration to them both! Nor do we need labor to make these items: no shearing, no spinning, no weaving, no sewing, no dyeing. There are so many creatures with so many designs and colors and patterns! You humans can't achieve the same quality in your work as is done in nature. And we don't have to dress our young for years on end, putting on their clothes every morning and stripping them off every evening; or washing, drying, mending and so on. The Creator has made it possible for us to rest from all such troubles. But you don't have this luxury.

Furthermore, the self-consciousness of which you boast actually counts for little. Remember that the Creator had intended you to be naked and carefree like us, but then Adam and Eve chose to follow their own rebellious inclinations. You wear clothes to cover your nakedness because in your twisted pride you have made yourselves ashamed of the very form you now boast about. Your bodies are indeed beautiful, but you cannot enjoy them without shame and secrecy—and you teach your young to feel the same. We animals, thankfully, are simple-hearted, not self-conscious. We are blessedly free from all that!"

VI

No sooner had Dragon, the spokes-carnivore, communicated these words, then Ka'as shouted out in anger: "How dare you talk to us of sin! You ought to be the ones embarrassed and ashamed! Among the animals there is none more evil than you, you family of carnivores! No one has greater strength and less usefulness! No one has less pity and mercy! No one is more voracious in eating than you!"

But Dragon retorted: "Before you humans were created, we carnivores didn't do these things and didn't hunt, because there was easily enough to sustain ourselves just from eating the corpses of the dead. Our ancestors didn't need to endanger themselves by hunting and killing. The lions, tigers, bears and their ilk found what they needed and were satisfied. But when you, the children of Adam and Eve, came and conquered the flocks and herds of the cloven-hooved ones, locked them behind fences and doors, and prevented them from returning to the wilderness, then we carnivores lacked their corpses and were forced to hunt among the living. And God permitted this, just as God first permitted you to eat dead and killed things to preserve your lives after the Great Flood, when food was lacking.

You mention our lack of mercy and the cruelty of our hearts—but behold—the other animals don't complain about us like they do about you! That's because they understand that we are not cruel, even though we do kill their weak and sick, their elderly and their young. We never kill for sport or profit; we never kill more than we need to survive. We are all part of the natural unity; what we do is but part of the Creator's design.

But you humans do not know yourselves as a part of this plan. You do not see yourselves as part of this natural unity. You kill the strongest and the most vital of us; you kill more than you need. You make yourselves fat at the expense of our lives. And worse, you do not even share our flesh with the poor and hungry of your own kind. It's true that we carnivores kill other animals—but that's nothing compared to the violence and harm that you've done to them, not to mention what evils you do against your own kind."

"How's that?" the King asked, perplexed. "You humans kill your own kind?"

The humans stood silent, downcast.

"Yes, that's absolutely true!" Dragon asserted. "You see human violence the world over; with their many wounded and dead being cast out, with the many others being sent into captivity and exile— the numbers cannot be counted! Humans do violence in everything! They fight for food and wealth and king and country—they even fight over God because each faith believes that it alone has the truth!

What are we compared to you humans?! But you glory in our shame and you say that we carnivores are the most evil creatures in the world. Why are you not ashamed that you disgrace yourselves in abusing not only us animals, but even your own kind?"

Then the entire assembly of spirits exclaimed: "Dragon is right in all he has said! If this is how you humans glorify yourselves, then your ignorance speaks against you. And as for what you have argued—why, it is all vanity, hot air, lies and fabrications!"

The hall erupted in roars and hoots, chirps and cheers. More sounds filled the court than have ever been heard in one place before or since.

The whole assembly of the humans was ashamed on that day. They were laid low, their cheeks burned and their heads hung down, all because the animals had triumphed. And, while the animals danced with glee and joy, there was much muttering in the human camp.

Zadone's voice had lost its malicious glow; Ga'avah was not so haughty; the usually hot-tempered Ka'as was subdued, and not even Ahzar's and Unf's hostile threats could keep everyone in line. Hochmah stood off to the side talking quietly with a number of others. A further awakening in her heart inspired a series of new thoughts to be explored, "Life is bigger than all of us. We are not at its center. It does not revolve around us, we are part of it. Do our egos and our appetites control our lives? Have we limited our goals to them? Are we robbing the earth of kindness, truth, and love? How are we going to change our ways?"

It was at this moment that the voice of the King was heard commanding: "Go in peace, each to his or her own place. Sleep there, and tomorrow return for judgment."

Upon hearing these words, Bersaf the Wise, King of the Spirits, arose from his throne, the seat of judgment, and he proclaimed: "If you humans would practice loving-kindness, the animals would work willingly alongside you. Heaven and earth would come together and gentle rain would fall. No one would need direction or instruction and all things would take their course. If you humans understood this, life would be transformed and all would be at peace. If you wish to rule, you must serve with humility.

GATE FIVE

The conclusion of the dispute between the humans
and all the seven classes of other living creatures, and
the verdict of King Bersaf

I

That night, the spirit sages met in the garden. The Master of Oaths and Incantations was speaking: "I never would have believed it possible! I owe you an apology, my brother from Adariss. I never thought the animals would best the humans in this debate."

"Nor did I, brother," replied the philosopher from Adariss, "but then who knew of the cloven-hooved ones' idea to seek outside assistance? It was a brilliant move and it saved the day, I'm sure. Now the only question is: What will the King decide to do? I am certain his verdict will be in favor of the animals—but how will he solve the larger problem? What redress will he give the animals? On the one hand, if he frees them, how will the humans survive, since it is apparent that their very survival depends on the animals in one way or another? On the other hand, would anything short of freedom be a just compensation for all the animals' suffering?"

II

The next morning, King Bersaf sat on his throne surrounded by his counselors and advisors. Before them stood the assembly of the seventy humans on one side, and the representatives of the seven classes of animals on the other side. The King looked towards the congregation of humans and reminded them: "You know what happened yesterday. The animals bested you with strong proofs. Nonetheless, I am still willing to entertain a final argument in defense of your claim. Do you have one?"

"My Lord and King," interjected the wisest of the spirit sages from Balakiss, "Before we proceed, I must point out that both parties have ignored something most important!"

"What is that?" the King asked in astonishment, a hint of annoyance in his words, as he was ready to finish the case.

Turning to those assembled, the spirit sage replied: "You families of humans and animals—you creatures of great matter, heavy bodies, bones and three dimensions—you know nothing about the multitude of spirit forms and fiery creations whose dwellings are in the space of the skies and who wander through the worlds of the spheres: from all kinds of angels, cherubim, seraphim, and shining beings who dwell in the seventh heaven, to the fiery spirits who dwell in the space of the sphere of the atmosphere, to the assemblies of spirits who dwell in the space of the sphere of the rains.

If you—you families of humans and animals—did comprehend the numbers and sorts that were created without matter and without dimensions—if you realized the multitude of our kinds and the infinite variations of our forms and visages—then this dispute between you two parties would be seen as the insignificant thing that it is. What do all these celestial and ethereal beings know or care about your little dispute? Creation is far greater than you can ever know, and you speak without understanding, you creatures who are but dust and ashes.

Remember God's questions to Eyov, whom some of you humans call Job:

> Where were you when God laid the earth's foundations?
> Speak if you have understanding.
> Do you know who fixed its dimensions
> Or who measured it with a line?
> Onto what were its bases sunk?
> Who set its cornerstone
> When the morning stars sang together
> And all the divine beings shouted for joy?

Have you penetrated to the sources of the sea,
Or walked in the recesses of the deep?
Have the gates of death been disclosed to you?
Have you seen the gates of deep darkness?
Have you surveyed the expanses of the earth?
If you know of these—tell me.

Once you stop to consider all the marvels of God, the One whom not even the wisest of creatures can wholly perceive, then you may begin to understand your place in creation!"

The spirit sage from Balakiss paused to let his words sink in, then he added: "If all that I've heard in this dispute represents your level of understanding of things—you families of humans and you families of animals—then surely you both are on the lower levels of creation. And all your arguments and counter arguments prove nothing, because we are all God's creations, we are all equally part of the Great Oneness. All that is asked of us is to treat one another with respect and loving-kindness!"

III

Then Tawadu, a man who had remained silent until now, took courage from the spirit sage's words. He pushed his way through the human assembly and came to stand in front of Unf and Ahzar and the other human speakers. "Although I am of small worth, I would like to respond to you both," he said meekly, looking at the King and his sage.

"Speak!" boomed the King, disregarding the astonished and hostile looks of Unf and Ahzar.

So Tawadu bravely spoke up in his quiet voice: "O spirit sage from Balakiss, your words are true and worthy of praise. There are humans who understand this. They are righteous people, pure and holy ones, sages, saints inspired with the Holy Spirit, prophets, and other messengers of God, all of whom follow the Way of loving-

71

kindness. The Creator appoints thirty-six of them in every generation to guide and sustain the world. When they die, their souls ascend to a dwelling place on high and others are born to take their places. You may not believe it based on what you've seen and heard in this case, but there are many among us who strive to follow their teachings."

As he spoke, a murmur began to ripple through the human assembly. One by one, various individuals began to voice support for what Tawadu was saying. Ahzar and Unf and their followers soon found themselves pushed to the back of the hall. There they slunk about dejectedly, and looked about for the exits, ready to make a quick retreat.

Tawadu continued: "However, I too have one proof for human superiority..." he began. Everyone looked at him in shock and silent horror but, before he could continue, a monstrous tumult erupted in the assembly in reaction to his words.

IV

When the King finally silenced the hall, and order was restored, Tawadu begged to continue.

"I have one proof for human superiority," he repeated softly, "which paradoxically is no proof at all. As a result of Adam and Eve's choice, we humans have been both blessed and cursed with a moral conscience. We alone know good from evil. We alone know if we follow God's Way or not. But here is the paradox: If we follow God's Way, if we listened to our moral conscience, then we would not act arrogantly and treat other living creatures as if they were our slaves and we their masters. Were we humans to obey our consciences—which we alone have—then paradoxically, we would not be so proud nor act so haughtily. All would be in equilibrium. So my proof of human superiority is no proof at all—see what I mean?"

Then the representatives of the animals and the all the sages of the King exclaimed as with one voice: "Now you've spoken the truth! This indeed is the way in which all humans should conduct themselves! But you humans, it isn't so with most of your kind! Look who your leaders were here... the Creator has given you gifts of wisdom and understanding—that is your glory—but your deeds should match your gifts!"

V

Upon hearing these words, Bersaf the Wise, King of the Spirits, arose from his throne, the seat of judgment, and he proclaimed: "If you humans would practice loving-kindness, the animals would work willingly *alongside* you. Heaven and earth would come together and gentle rain would fall. No one would need direction or instruction and all things would take their course. If you humans understood this, life would be transformed and all would be at peace.

If you wish to rule, you must serve with humility. If you choose to lead, you must learn what it means to follow. In this way, when you rule, the animals will not feel oppressed and they will not be harmed. The whole world will support you and not tire of you. Do you think you can rule the world and actually improve it? I, Bersaf, do not believe it can be done. The world is sacred. You cannot improve it. Ultimately, you can only change yourselves.

The Creator's providence gives all things life. All God's creatures are nourished by it and so all revere God and seek to follow God's Way. They want to do this because it is natural for them. How does The Creator's providence give them life and rear them? It nurses them on loving-kindness, brings them to maturity, feeds and shelters them.

Therefore, o humans, heed my words: cultivate loving-kindness in yourselves. Cultivate it in your families. Cultivate it in your settlements. Cultivate it in your nations. Cultivate it in the world and it will be everywhere."

Then Bersaf the King declared: "Now I will deliver my verdict."

VI

And all the King's advisors and the spirit sages, all the representatives of the humans, and all the emissaries of the animals rose up and stood silently awaiting his words.

"By the grace of God, I find myself in favor of the animals, for they have been sorely tested and abused. However, it is clear to me that these humans now realize the harm they have caused to God's other creations and now begin to understand more of what it means to be rulers. Therefore, although I find in favor of the animals in their lawsuit—the humans are guilty for what they have done up until now—nonetheless I decree that the animals shall remain subject to human control as before. But this does not mean that things can remain as they were before this trial. You humans are hereby served notice that your behavior towards your fellow creatures must change! And to ensure your compliance with this court's decision, I am sending a record of these proceedings to the Supreme Court on High.

Furthermore, acting as agent of that Court on High, I am setting ten signs as warnings to you lest you backslide. If these things begin to occur, know that you had better change course and return to the Creator's Way lest catastrophe overtake you.

Should you err, the animals will begin to disappear, one by one, forever, from the face of the earth; and the air in your settlements and fortresses will become dangerous to breathe.

Should you still not change, the sky will weaken and the earth will reveal its nakedness to the sun; the water in your streams and the rain in the sky slowly will turn undrinkable.

Persevere in your wicked ways and still worse will happen: the seasons will be reversed and your climates turned on end; the earth will cease yielding up its goodness and the sky will cease its rain. In the middle of summer, plants will drop their leaves and unripe fruits will fall as if it were autumn.

Nor shall this be the end. Continue, and the animals you eat—fish and fowl, beast and bug—will bring sicknesses and death upon you, and you will be forced to fight each other—and even eat each other—for lack of food.

In the end, should you ignore all these previous signs—so help me God—you humans will be displaced from your place of glory and no longer rule the earth.

So mark my words, you humans, and heed my warning. Change your ways while there is yet time.

O humans, God set Adam and Eve on this earth as an act of goodness, charging them and their descendants to care for it and tend it. Creation is good; you can be good. So cease this ferocity toward your fellow creatures. Things need not turn out as I have said.

For now, let me simply remind you of your duty: You have domesticated some of the beasts and now that they are used to shelter and a regular supply of water and grains, they could not survive again in the wild. You humans have responsibility for them and you will be held accountable for the health and vitality of the domesticated creatures. You ought not rule them, but serve them, so that they might serve you better. The beasts are simple-hearted. In time they may come to trust you again if you carry your task out well.

This is my verdict, as God is my witness."

The humans stood in stunned silence, contemplating the weight of the fearsome curses and picturing what life would be like if the King's prophecy were to come about, but no one could muster a response, not even a word. All stood as mutes, with heads bowed.

VII

Finally Hochmah, that wise and sagacious woman, came forward to stand next to Tawadu. Then she prayed and confessed: "Praise to the Ruler of All Worlds, the Source of being and Giver of life to us all. What you say is true, our Lord and King, and your judgment is just. We have done wrong and we will try to do better. We must choose our leaders wisely and not surrender to crude anger, violence, and power." She pointedly looked about her, but Zadone and Unf, Ahzar and Ka'as, were nowhere to be seen.

Zadone, Unf, Ahzar, Ka'as and their gang had failed to convince the Court; they had failed to intimidate their fellow humans; they had even been bested by the beasts. Their hearts grew hard and dry. As they slunk from the hall in disgrace, their souls withered in bitterness because they chose to reject the divine blessings that flowed to every form of life present there. And suddenly, they were gone…

Then Hochmah continued: "Our sages and teachers have toiled to make the Creator's teachings clear, but they have never been completely able to succeed. In truth, language is insufficient and incapable of interpreting and explaining God's Way adequately. But, each in his or her own way, makes the same point over and over again: God is One, creation is one, all life is one. And when one part of that whole suffers, all of it eventually will suffer. Practicing loving-kindness restores wholeness and builds unity. Thus, we should always have this essential unity and wholeness in mind. My Lord and King, you bands of spirit sages, and you families of animals, we shall try to live our lives differently."

And all the humans remaining in the court chanted as with one voice: "As God is our witness! Amen and amen!"

Then Hochmah continued: *"Our sages and teachers have toiled to make God's teachings clear, but they have never been completely able to succeed. In truth, language is insufficient and incapable of interpreting and explaining God's Way adequately. But, each in his or her own way, makes the same point over and over again: God is One, creation is one, all life is one. And when one part of that whole suffers, all of it eventually will suffer. Practicing loving-kindness restores wholeness and builds unity. Thus, we should always have this essential unity and wholeness in mind. My Lord and King, you bands of spirit sages, and you families of animals, we shall try to live our lives differently."*

At that moment, the earth gently began to rock as if cradling a baby, the wind whispered in the ears of the all those assembled, and a diffuse light shone down softly on every creature in the court. Flowers opened up to the light emanating from the sky, and tiny drops of gentle rain fell on everyone. As the humans beheld this wonder, their hearts opened to the warmth and light and moisture, and seeds of compassion were sown in this fertile earth. For these welcoming, wondering souls, their hearts became filled with loving-kindness, and their love and understanding grew. A new appreciation of life grew within them. They felt a living light spreading in each of them, healing the sin that had once blinded them to the common divine origin that they share with all other living things. They gazed upon one another with loving-kindness, as if through eyes of the Holy One, and they felt God's presence bless their lives with God's own goodness…

Then the remaining humans, now freed from the grasp of violence, pride, and deceit, together with all the animals, praised the wise words of the King and all accepted his verdict. To commemorate the occasion, and to mark the newly-made pact between the humans and the animals, Hochmah the Wise Woman and Nightingale composed and performed this song:

Let the seas sing out in thunderous voice
While the sky and the earth together rejoice
Let the mountain peaks chant a joyous song
And the rivers clap hands, a happy throng.
When the great forest trees dance and sway,
Hear what the wild winds have to say.

There was an isle in the Sea of Green
Tsagone by name, a place unseen,
Where all the animals lived in peace,
The lion, the lamb, the tiger, the beast.
Until one day a ship was lost,
Humans on its shores were tossed.

They built up shops and farms and homes,
Enslaved the animals, made them groan.
The beasts complained to the Spirit King,
 And to his Court a letter did bring.
"What is our crime? What is our guilt?
Will you allow our blood to be spilt?"

Bersaf the King, awesome to see,
Heard their tale of tragedy.
He summoned the humans to come and explain
Why they burdened the beasts and caused them such pain.
The humans replied: "It's our God-given right,
To use the animals all day and all night."

The beasts sent messengers to all of their kind:
"Send help right away, or no peace will we find!
These humans cause us much trouble and sorrow,
We need help at once or there'll be no tomorrow!
They say we're slaves, they say they're our master
If you don't speak up, we'll all suffer disaster!"

To the aid of the beasts, the creatures came calling,
Some flying, some swimming, some running,
        some crawling.
The parrot, the bee, the goggle-eyed frog,
The cricket, the dragon—the Court was agog
To see such an endless variety of creatures
A myriad of forms! Such beauteous features!

The animals addressed the Court one by one:
"Look, our King, how much harm they have done!
The beasts they raise are not just for meat,
They work them so hard that death appears sweet!
Did not the one God create us all?
What makes them think they stand so tall?"

Each presented its case and argued with pride,
But the humans were clever, not to mention most snide.

"You animals know nothing! We're smarter than you!
We make things and bake things—what do you do?
We have thinkers who write and cleaners who sweep,
You're just instinctive; you eat and you sleep."

"Which means that our talents are borne innate
While yours take years to inculcate.
Our young are wise from the moment of birth
But yours spend years learning value and worth.
We live simply, our lives are thus blessed—
But all your knowledge just leaves you distressed."

"Consider our builders"—"Well what of the ant?
It builds without tools, that's something you can't!"
"You eat one another"—"And you kill and quarrel
Disputing allegedly God-given morals!"
"But we alone know good from bad..."
"That is precisely what makes us so mad!

To know but choose wrongly, that is your sin.
Pray see all the woe that your sin's put us in!"
The King listened well; but how to decide
When both claimed God supported their side?
The humans, t'was clear, had the power to rule,
But they didn't know how, they were much too cruel.

Said Bersaf: "O beasts, you've suffered great losses,
Can you ever forgive them for being harsh bosses?"
Said the King to the humans: "God created you last,
So your knowledge is lacking; you'd better learn fast:
Take care! Beware! Or this earth you'll destroy!
God made you to rule, good sense to employ.

Treat living things kindly; all cruelty do cease;
Strive to live better. Now, please, go in peace!"
The humans heard well what the wise King had said
If they didn't comply, they could all end up dead!
What is Creation, if not one living whole?
To live and let live—that is the goal!

To mark the occasion, a covenant was made
That none on earth should again be afraid.
Then hand took hoof and claw and wing,
And under the trees all the living did sing:
"The earth is the Lord's and all that it holds..."
Thus ends our story; our tale's now told.

Let the seas sing out in thunderous voice
While the sky and the earth together rejoice
Let the mountain peaks chant a joyous song
And the rivers clap hands, a happy throng.
When the great forest trees dance and sway,
Hear what the wild winds have to say.
(music by Nightingale; lyrics by Hochmah Human)

As Bersaf the Wise, King of the spirits, heard their pleasant harmonies and their clever rendition of the controversy, he glowed orange with contentment and blue with pleasure. Then Bersaf the King, pure and honest, God-fearing and shunning evil, hospitable to guests, defender of the poor, merciful toward the unfortunate, a dispenser of gifts and charity, far-removed from oppression, despising iniquity, opposing villainy with great conviction and with great anger—there isn't another like him in all creation!—he arose and declared: "May God bless you all, each and every one! Now go, all of you, and return to your homes in peace! This court is adjourned."

And so, with prayers and praise, songs and psalms, they went, each to its own kind, and all dwelt in peace.

CONCLUDING PRAYER
BY THE ORIGINAL AUTHORS OF THIS TALE

And this concludes the tale of the animals' lawsuit against humanity, one of fifty-one treatises in which we tell the wisdoms of ages
and examine the many aspects of existence. May the Creator enable you, our brothers and our sisters, to read and understand the
teachings in this tale, and the secrets which are scattered in all fifty-
one tracts, so that your hearts are open to its message and you learn
to act as you should, for this alone is what the Creator wants. Amen.

And this completes the retelling of this tale by us, Anson Laytner
and Dan Bridge, Matthew Kaufmann, and Kulsum Begum, in the
year 5765 of the Jewish counting, in the year 1425 of the Islamic
counting, or 2004 in the Common Era.

THE END

And so, with prayers and praise, songs and psalms, they went, each to its own kind, and all dwelt in peace.

AFTERWORD

The Torah contains a number of important concepts regarding the proper treatment of animals (and people too for that matter) that are still highly relevant today. Furthermore, since the Hebrew Bible (which Jews call the Tanakh) is the foundation upon which Rabbinic Judaism, Christianity, and Islam all are built, what it teaches also has implications for adherents of all three traditions.

Primary among these concepts is *hesed*, a Hebrew word that is central to our story. The word has implications of loving-kindness, compassion, and faithfulness, with overtones of righteousness thrown in. *Hesed* traditionally is seen as one of God's operating principles in Creation, along with justice, and mercy, righteousness and judgment, as, for example, in this excerpt from Psalm 96: "God will rule the earth justly and its peoples with loving-kindness (*hesed*)". *Hesed* is God's to manifest and ours to emulate. Thus, in Jewish tradition, there is a whole category of commandments, called deeds of loving-kindness (*gemillut hasadim*), through which we act compassionately to others and by which we strive to imitate God's behavior. In our tale, *hesed* is the quality that the humans need to discover in themselves in order to reconnect with the natural world and with other living creatures in particular.

Following God's way of *hesed* begins with our acknowledgement that God is the Source of all Creation and the recognition that all we use, even to our very lives, is a gift of divine love. Therefore, our sages taught that it is forbidden to enjoy (or use) something in this world without first offering a blessing of gratitude—to do otherwise would be to misappropriate sacred property. On this point, opinion is fairly uniform. However, when it comes to understanding our place in Creation, opinions divide, as in our story, over whether humankind is to dominate or to co-exist.

Not surprisingly, whether or not one eats animals is central to understanding this issue. It all hinges on how one interprets God's command, in Genesis 1, to the primordial parents, Adam and Eve, and then God's commandment to Noah after the flood (Genesis 9). In Genesis 1, God gives people every seed-bearing plant and every tree with seed-bearing fruit for food, while after the Flood, the eating of meat is permitted. One could argue that being carnivores was not part of God's original plan but only a concession to and acknowledgement of human behavior. However, even after allowing the eating of meat, God imposes certain criteria on this cruel cuisine: Noah is told not to eat flesh with its life-blood in it, which the rabbis understood to mean that one should not cut a limb from a living creature to eat. That would be too cruel. Indeed, one can view the entire system of keeping kosher (and other "ritual" commandments) as an attempt to channel our "natural" or "wild" instincts in more constructive and uplifting directions. Thus, for example, instead of eating anything that lives, Torah restricts what Jews may eat; instead of killing animals any which way for food, Torah dictates a (relatively) humane way of slaughter accompanied by a prayer. In these sorts of ways, we are directed to remember the Source of our food and to be more aware of that Source in all that we do.

From this perspective, "right diet" and "right action" are ways of promoting "right intention" in seeking to follow God's path of *hesed*. There are also two specific commandments in the Torah that can help guide a person in the way of *hesed*: *bal tashkhit* and *tsa'ar baalei hayyim*, meaning "do not destroy" and "afflicting animals" respectively.

In the Torah, "do not destroy" is a principle in warfare. It reluctantly accepts that wars will be fought, but seeks to impose moral standards on combat, one of which is not to needlessly destroy the land when one is at war. In other words, if you battle, remember it is other people whom you are fighting, do not wage war against the trees and crops and animals of that land too. They are innocent—not to mention that after the battle, they will be needed again to sustain human life. As a general environmental principle, "do not destroy" means use what you need, use wisely, do not waste, save something for the future.

The second commandment, "afflicting animals" prohibits causing any living creature needless pain. Here too Torah recognizes that people use animals to work their farms, carry their loads, and for their food and clothing. In our tale, the animals' chief complaint is not so much that this is their fate but that we humans abuse them, that is, we don't treat them with *hesed*. Consequently, as with "do not destroy", Torah tries to put some moral guidelines to our use of animals—like feeding them before we feed ourselves, not yoking together animals of different strengths and abilities, not overloading or overworking them, not killing a mother and its young together and, perhaps most important of all, not causing them pain, particularly if we must slaughter them for food.

Finally, there is the Jewish mystical concept of *tikkun olam*, mentioned in the preface to this story. According to the traditional idea, the vessels of Creation could not contain God's divine light and so they shattered, causing divine sparks to scatter everywhere. Part of humanity's job thus became to help God "repair the world" by gathering up these divine sparks. For Jews, this means to live our lives to the best of our abilities according to God's will (the commandments). Thus, from this perspective, every good deed, every act of loving-kindness—how we treat the natural world, how we treat other living things, and how we treat one another—are not just intrinsically good deeds, they also help bring the world closer to redemption one spark at a time.

JEWISH SOURCES

On *Hesed* and Creation

God's compassion extends to all of Creation.
> Psalm 145:9

Our Rabbis taught: Even those things that you may regard as completely superfluous to Creation—such as fleas, gnats, and flies—even they too were included in Creation; and God's purpose is carried out through everything—even through a snake, a scorpion, a gnat, or a frog.
> Midrash Genesis Rabbah, 10:7
> Land of Israel, c. 400 CE

What is the way that will lead to the proper love and fear of God? When you contemplate God's great, wondrous works and creatures, and from them obtain a glimpse of divine wisdom, incomparable and infinite, you will straightway love God, praise God, glorify God, and long with an exceeding longing to know God's great name, even as David said, *Like a deer crying for water/My soul cries for You, O God/My soul thirsts for God, the living God* (Psalms 42:2-3). And you, who ponder these matters will recoil, frightened with the realization of being a small creature, lowly and obscure…And so David (also) said: *When I behold Your heavens, the work of Your fingers/The moon and stars that You have set in place/What is humankind that you are mindful of it?* (Psalm 8:4-5)
> Mishneh Torah, Book of Knowledge, 2:2
> Rambam (Rabbi Moses Maimonides)
> Egypt, 1135-1204 CE

Our task must be to free ourselves…by widening our circle of compassion to embrace all living creatures and the whole of nature and its beauty.
> Albert Einstein
> Germany / America 20th C.

One glorious chain of love, of giving and receiving, unites all living things. All things exist in continuous reciprocal activity—one for All, All for one. None has power, or means, for itself; each receives only in order to give, and gives in order to receive, and finds therein the fulfillment of the purpose of its existence: HaShem (YHWH/ the Lord). "Love," say the Sages, "love that supports and is supported in turn. That is the character of the Universe."

> The Nineteen Letters, 3rd letter (end)
> Rabbi Samson Raphael Hirsch
> Germany, 1808-1888

Against "Afflicting Animals" (*Tsaar Baalei Hayyim*)

Rav Judah said that Rav said: A person is forbidden to eat before the domesticated animals have been given food, for Scripture (first) says: *I will provide grass in the fields for your cattle*, and only then it says: *and you shall eat your fill* (Deuteronomy 11:15).

> Talmud of Babylonia, Berakhot 40a; Gittin 62a
> c. 200-600 CE

The sufferings of Rabbi (Judah the Patriarch) came to him because of a certain incident and left in the same way. What was the incident that led to his suffering? Once a calf was being taken to slaughter when it broke away, hid its head under Rabbi's robes, and bellowed (in terror). Rabbi said, "Go! For this is why you were created!" Then they said in heaven, "Since he showed no compassion, let us bring suffering upon him." And how did Rabbi's suffering depart? One day a slave was sweeping the house and was about to sweep away some young weasels. "Leave them alone!" Rabbi said. "It is written: *God's compassion extends to all of Creation.* Then they said in heaven, "Since he has shown compassion, let us be compassionate with him."

> Babylonian Talmud, Baba Metzia, 85a
> c. 200-600 CE

Scripture placed domestic and wild animals on a par with humans with regard to food, and did not permit humans to kill any creature and eat its flesh; rather, all of them alike were to eat vegetation. But later, from the time of Noah's children, God permitted people and animals to eat meat.

> Rashi (Rabbi Solomon ben Isaac)
> Torah Commentary to Genesis 1:29-31
> France, 1040 – 1105 CE

Your compassion should encompass all creatures, not destroying or despising them, for Wisdom on high encompasses all created things—minerals, plants, animals, and human beings! This is the reason behind the Rabbis warning us about lack of respect for our sources of food (TB, Berakhot 50b). Because Wisdom on high disrespects nothing—everything being derived from there, as it is written: *You have made them all via Wisdom* (Psalms 104.24). It is fitting that our compassion should also take in all God's works…Thus, you should not uproot anything that grows, nor kill any living thing unless it is needed (for food). And you should choose a quick and easy death for them, with a knife carefully inspected, to have compassion on them as far as possible. To sum up: The principle of Wisdom is that love should be extended to everything that exists, so that you do not harm them but rather elevate them ever higher, from plant to animal and from animal to human. For only then it is permitted to uproot the plant or to kill the beast, to transform a loss into a gain.

> Tomer Devorah (Deborah's Palm Tree) 3 (end)
> Rabbi Moses Cordovero
> Land of Israel, 1522-1570

One rabbinic legal opinion has it that one should not recite a blessing over (new) shoes or clothes made of leather, for the animal might have been killed solely to produce this item and, as the verse says, "God's compassion extends to all of Creation". Now such reasoning is weak and inconclusive, yet many are careful not to say the blessing.

> Gloss to Rabbi Joseph Karo's Opinion
> Rabbi Moses Isserles
> Poland, d. 1572

The law against afflicting animals (with pain and suffering) applies in every case, except where an animal is slaughtered outright or killed for a material benefit to human beings.

> Nodah bi-Yehudah, Yoreh Deah, second series, 10
> Rabbi Ezekiel Landau
> Bohemia, 1713-1793

Do Not Destroy (*Bal Tashkhit*)

When you besiege a city for a long time—making war against it in order to take it—you shall not destroy its trees by wielding an axe against them. You may eat from them, but you must not cut them down! Are trees of the field human beings to withdraw before you into the besieged city? Only trees that you know are not food-bearing you may destroy and cut down in order to build siege-works...

> Deuteronomy 20:19-20

Not only one who cuts down food trees, but also one who smashes household goods, tears clothes, demolishes a building, stops up a spring, or destroys food on purpose violates the command: "*You must not destroy.* Such a person is administered a disciplinary beating.

> Mishneh Torah, Book of Judges,
> Laws of Kings and Wars, 6:10
> Rambam (Rabbi Moses Maimonides)
> Egypt, 1135-1204

The prohibition of purposeless destruction of food trees around a besieged city is only to be taken as an example of general wastefulness. Under the concept of bal tash-chit (You must not destroy), the purposeless destruction of anything at all is taken to be forbidden, so that our text becomes the most comprehensive warning to human beings not to misuse the position that God has given them as master of the world and its matter by capricious, passionate, or merely thoughtless wasteful destruction of anything on earth.

> Horeb: Essays on Israel's "Duties" in the Diaspora
> Rabbi Samson Raphael Hirsch
> Germany, 1837

REPAIR OF THE WORLD (*Tikkun Olam*)

God said, "I will make humankind in My image, after My likeness. They shall rule...the whole earth..." (Genesis 1:28) Rabbi Hanina said: "If humankind merits it, God says 'rule!'; but if humankind does not merit it, God says 'Let them (the animals) rule!'"

> Midrash Genesis Rabbah 8:12
> Land of Israel, c. 400 CE

Said Dov Baer, the Preacher of Mezhirech (Ukraine): Your kind deeds are used by God as seed for the planting of trees in the Garden of Eden. Thus, each of you creates your own Paradise.

> Esser Orot (Ten Lights)
> Ukraine, d. 1772

When God created the first human beings, God led them around the Garden of Eden and said: "Look at My works! See how beautiful they are—how excellent! For you sake I created them all. See to it that you do not spoil and destroy My world; for if you do, there will be no one else to repair it."

> Midrash Ecclesiastes Rabbah 1 on Ecclesiastes 7:13
> c. 800 CE

Jewish selections from *A Garden of Choice Fruits: 200 Classic Jewish Quotes on Human Beings and the Environment*, edited and designed by Rabbi David E. Stein, Wyncote, PA: Shomrei Adamah/Keepers of the Earth, 1991.

ISLAMIC SOURCES

Within the tenets of Islam are found strong support and guidelines for the protection and treatment of animals.

In the Qur'an and Hadith (sayings of the Prophet), it is emphasized that animals be treated as humanely as any other of God's vast creation. The Qur'an goes as far to say that cruelty to animals is equivalent to cruel treatment of a human being. Kind treatment of animals is considered a good deed in the same sense that good conduct and treatment between human beings is deemed a good deed. The following Hadith illustrates this point:

> The Prophet said, "While a man was walking he felt thirsty and went down a well, and drank water from it. On coming out of it, he saw a dog panting and eating mud because of excessive thirst. The man said, 'This (dog) is suffering from the same problem as that of mine.' So, he (went down the well), filled his shoe with water, caught hold of it with his teeth and climbed up and watered the dog. Allah thanked him for his (good) deed and forgave him." The people asked "O Allah's Apostle! Is there a reward for us in serving (the) animals?" He replied: "Yes, there is a reward for serving any animate (living being)."
> Narrated by Abu Huraira
> Volume 3, Book 40, Number 551

God created man to be the guardian of the Earth and gave him dominion over its inhabitants. Therefore, mankind is held responsible for an injustice he has done to any of God's creatures. The Qur'an specifies that animals function as a community in the same way that human beings do, and all creatures have their place. The Qur'an also shows that it is not only human beings that give praise and worship to God through prayers but animals as well, as evident from this passage.

"Seest thou not that it is Allah Whose praises are celebrated by all beings in the heavens and on earth, and by the birds with extended wings? Each one knows its prayer and psalm, And Allah is aware of what they do."

Qur'an 22:18

It says in another Hadith narrated from Ibn Abbas that the Prophet said "Do not use anything in which there is a soul as a target."

Narrated by Muslim

In Islam, the Qur'an and Hadith give clear guidance on several matters concerning animals, aside from their treatment and roles. Another issue which is carefully described in the Qur'an and Hadith is the slaughter of animals for food. In Islam, one must follow strict guidelines from the Qur'an and Hadith on the process and proper way of slaughter.

From *Animals in Islam* by Anayat Durrani

***

The sources quoted in *Animals in Islam* by Al-Hafiz B. A. Masri are the Qur'an, the first source of Islamic law (*Shari'ah*); Hadith or Tradition, the second source; and Ijtihad, inference by analogy, the third source. Together, these three sources make up Islamic case law or "Juristic Rules" that are the guidelines to be followed for any legal question. Many issues relating to animals, such as vivisection, factory farming, and animal rights did not exist 14 centuries ago and therefore, no specific laws were passed about them. To decide on issues developed in recent times, Islamic Jurisprudence (*fiqh*) has left it to Muslim Jurists (*fuqaha'a*) to use their judgement by inference and analogy, based on the three above-mentioned sources.

DOMINION OVER ANIMALS

The Qur'an states that man has dominion over animals: "He (God) it is Who made you vicegerents on earth." (Qur'an 35:39), but makes clear that this responsibility is not unconditional and states what happens to those who misuse their freedom of choice and fail to conform to the conditions that limit this responsibility: "then We reduce him (to the status of) the lowest of the low." (Qur'an 95:4,5) "...they are those whom Allah has rejected and whom He has condemned....because they served evil" (Qur'an 5:63). "...they have hearts wherewith they fail to comprehend, and eyes wherewith they fail to see, and ears wherewith they fail to hear....Such (humans) are far astray from the right path.

> Qur'an 7:179

There are...people who take the concept of man's dominion over animals as a licentious freedom to break all the established moral rules designed to protect animal rights. The Imam Hazrat Ali has this to say about (those who misuse their authority over the weak): "A savage and ferocious beast is better than a wicked and tyrant ruler."

> Maxims, see Ref. No. 4, pp. 203, 381

ANIMALS ARE OUR TEACHERS

Muslims have often been advised by their mentors to learn lessons from some species of animal. For example, the Imam Hazrat Ali gives this piece of advice: "Be like a bee; anything he eats is clean, anything he drops is sweet and any branch he sits upon does not break."

> Maxims of Ali; translated by Al-Halal from Nahj-ul-Balagha (in Arabic); Sh. Muhammad Ashraf, Lahore, Pakistan; p. 436. The Imam, Hazrat Ali bin Abi Talib was the son-in-law of the Holy Prophet Muhammad(s), and the fourth Caliph (644–656 A.C. = 23–24 A.H.

ANIMALS ARE MEMBERS OF COMMUNITIES AND THE FAMILY OF GOD

The Holy Prophet Muhammad(s) puts it in these words: "All creatures are like a family (Ayal) of God: and he loves the most those who are the most beneficent to His family.

> Narrated by Anas. Mishkat al-Masabih,3:1392; quoted from Bukhari.

The Qur'an states: "There is not an animal on earth, nor a bird that flies on its wings, but they are communities like you…"

Qur'an 6:38

The Holy Prophet(s) used to say· "Whoever is kind to the creatures of God, is kind to himself."

Wisdom of Prophet Mohammad(s); Muhammad Amin; The Lion Press, Lahore, Pakistan; 1945.

According to the learned commentators of the Qur'an "…animals all live a life, individual and social, like members of a human commune. Even those species which are generally considered as insignificant or even dangerous deserve to be treated as communities; that their intrinsic and not perceptible values should be recognized, irrespective of their usefulness or their apparent harmfulness."

"Verily God is not ashamed to speak of the gnat."

Qu'ran, The Cow, Surah al-Baqarah 2:26

Abu Huraira reported the Prophet(s) as telling of an incident that happened to another prophet in the past. This prophet was stung by an ant and, in anger, he ordered the whole of the ants' nest to be burned. At this, God reprimanded this prophet in these words: 'because one ant stung you, you have burned a whole community which glorified Me'. (Bukhari and Muslim).

The Islamic law (Shari'ah) concerning the rights of animals are very elaborate and explicit. In the case of the ants' nest, the following Juristic Rule would apply: Any damage or a damaging retaliation for a damage is forbidden. (*La zarara wa la zirar*).

PROVIDING FOR ANIMALS USED TO CARRY HEAVY LOADS

Animals in the service of man should be used only when necessary and their comfort should not be neglected

Saying daily prayers (*salat*) is one of the five most important obligations of the Muslim religion. In the following Hadith, one of his companions tells us that the Holy Prophet(s) and his fellow travelers used to delay even saying their prayers until they had first given their riding and pack animals fodder and had attended to their needs: "When we stopped at a halt, we did not say our prayers until we had taken the burdens off our camels' backs and attended to their needs."

> Narrated by Anas. Awn (Ref. No. 32); 7:223; Hadith aNo. 5234. Also 'Guillaume' (Ref. No. 57); pp.106, 107

CRUELTY TO ANIMALS

According to the spirit and overall teachings of Islam, causing unavoidable pain and suffering to the defenseless and innocent creatures of God is not justifiable under any circumstances. Islam wants us to think and act in the positive terms of accepting all species as communities like us in their own right and not to sit in judgement on them according to our human norms and values.

Prevention of physical cruelty is not enough; mental cruelty is equally important. In the following incident, a bird's emotional distress has been treated as seriously as a physical injury:

> We were on a journey with the Apostle of God(s), and he left us for a while. During his absence, we saw a bird called hummara with its two young and took the young ones. The mother bird was circling above us in the air, beating its wings in grief, when the Prophet came back and said: 'Who has hurt the FEELINGS of this bird by taking its young? Return them to her'.
> Narrated by Abdul Rahman bin Abdullah bin Mas'ud. Muslim. Also Awn (Ref. No. 32) Hadith No. 2658. Also "Guillaume' (Ref. No. 57); p. 106).

It is reported by the same authority that: "a man once robbed some eggs from the nest of a bird. The Prophet(s) had them restored to the nest." (id).

The Islamic concern about cruelty to animals is so great that it has declared the infliction of any unnecessary and avoidable pain 'even to a sparrow or any creature smaller than that' as a sin for which the culprit would be answerable to God on the Day of Judgement.

The Holy Prophet(s) has even tried the 'Punishment and Reward' approach as recorded in the following hadith:

> The Prophet(s) told his companions of a woman who would be sent to Hell for having locked up a cat; not feeding it, nor even releasing it so that it could feed herself.
>
> Narrated by Abdullah bin 'Omar. Bukhari, 4:337; recorded in Riyad (Ref. No. 28), Hadith No. 1605; p. 271. Also Muslim, Vol. 4, Hadith No. 2242. English translation by Abdul Hamid Siddiqi; Sh. Muhammad Ashraf, Lahore, Pakistan; 1976; Vol. 4, Hadith No. 5570; p. 1215. (According to the English translation, this Hadith was also narrated by the Abu Huraira and by Naqi who had heard it from Abdullah); Hadith No. 5573; p. 1215.) This Hadith has been recorded by almost all the authentic books of hadith, as the Re. No. 53 will show.)

Islam's concern for animals goes beyond the prevention of physical cruelty or even condescending kindness to them, which is a negative proposition. It enjoins on the human species, as the principle primates of the animated world, to take over the responsibility of all creatures in the spirit of a positive philosophy of life and to be their active protectors.

The Prophet(s) was asked if acts of charity even to the animals were rewarded by God. He replied: "Yes, there is a reward for acts of charity to every beast alive."

> Narrated by Abu Huraira, Bukhari, 3:322. Also Muslim, Vol. 4; Hadith No. 2244. Also Awn (Ref. No. 32), 7:222, Hadith No. 2533. Also Mishkat al-masabih, Book 6; Chapter 6.

Mishkat Al-Masabih concluded from the transmitters of prophetic sayings, Bukhari and Muslim, that: "A good deed done to a beast is as good as doing good to a human being; while an act of cruelty to a beast is as bad as an act of cruelty to human beings' and that: 'Kindness to animals was promised by rewards in Life Hereafter."

> Mishkat al-Masabih; Book 6; Chapter 7, 8:178.

ANIMALS HAVE CONSCIOUSNESS

Many passages from the Qur'an and Ahadith state that all animals are endowed with spirit and mind and "…there is ample evidence in the Qur'an to suggest that animals' consciousness of spirit and mind is of a degree higher than mere instinct and intuition. We are told in the Qur'an that animals have a cognizance of their Creator and, hence, they pay their obeisance to Him by adoration and worship: Seest thou not that it is Allah Whose praises are celebrated by all beings in the heavens and on earth, and by the birds with extended wings? Each one knows its prayer and psalm, And Allah is aware of what they do.
Qur'an 24:41

It is worth noting the statement that 'each one knows its prayer and psalm'. The execution of a voluntary act, performed consciously and intentionally, requires a faculty higher than that of instinct and intuition. Lest some people should doubt that animals could have such a faculty, the following verse points out that it is human ignorance that prevents them from understanding this phenomenon: The seven heavens and the earth and all things therein declare His glory. There is not a thing but celebrates His adoration; and yet ye mankind! ye understand not how do they declare His glory….
Qur'an 17:44

ANIMALS AND HUMANS MUST SHARE NATURAL RESOURCES

Once it has been established that each species of animal is a "community" like the human community, it stands to reason that each and every creature on earth has, as its birth-right, a share in all the natural resources. In other words, each animal is a tenant-in-common on this Planet with human species.

The Qur'an repeatedly emphasizes that food and other resources of nature are there to be shared equitably with other creatures. Below are just a few of numerous such verses: Then let man look at his food: how We pour out water in showers, then turn up the earth into furrow-slices and cause cereals to grow therein—grapes and green fodder, olive-trees and palm-trees, and luxuriant orchards,

fruits and grasses…as Provision for you as well as for your cattle.
Qur'an 80:24-32

Again, in the following verses, the bounties of nature are enumerated with the accent on animals' share in all of them. Everything was created for human AND non-human animals: And He it is Who sends the winds, as glad tidings heralding His mercy. And We send down pure water from the clouds, that We may give life thereby, by watering the parched earth, and slake the thirst of those We have created—both the animals and the human beings in multitude.
Qur'an 25-48,49

And the earth: He {God} has assigned to all living creatures.
Qur'an 55:10

The essence of Islamic teachings on 'Animal Rights' is that depriving animals of their fair share in the resources of nature is so serious a sin in the eyes of God that it is punishable by punitive retribution: The Qur'an describes how the people of Thamud demanded that the Prophet Saleh(s) show them some sign to prove he was a prophet of God. (The tribe of Thamud were the descendants of Noah. They have also been mentioned in the Ptolemaic records of Alexander's astronomer of the 2nd century A.C.)

At the time of this incident, the tribe was experiencing a dearth of food and water and was, therefore, neglecting its livestock. It was revealed to Prophet Saleh(s) to single out a she-camel as a symbol and ask his people to give her her fair share of water and fodder. The people of Thamud promised to do that but, later, killed the camel. As a retribution, the tribe was annihilated. This incident has been mentioned in the Qur'an many times in different contexts.
Qur'an 7:73, 11:64, 26:155, 156; 54:27-31

Experimentation on Animals

Needs are classified in three categories: necessities (al-Masalih ad-darurfyah) without which life could not be sustained; needs required for comfort and easement from pain or any kind of distress, or for improving the quality of life (*al-Masalih-al-haiya*); and luxuries (*al-Masalih at tahsiniyah*) desirable for enjoyment or self-indulgence.

Some rules that can be applied to these needs to determine whether experiments on animals would be allowed: What allures to the forbidden, is itself forbidden. (*Ma'ad'a ela al-harame, fahuwaharamun*). This rule implies that material gains, including food, obtained by wrongful acts, such as unnecessary experiments on animals, become unlawful (*haram*).

No damage can be put right by a similar or a greater damage. (*Ad-dararu la yuzalu be mislehi au be dararin akbaro minho*). When we damage our health and other interests by our own follies, we have no right to make the animals pay for it by inflicting similar or greater damage on them, such as by doing unnecessary experiments to find remedies for our self-induced ailments.

Resort to alternatives, when the original becomes undesirable. (*Iza ta'zuro al-aslu, yusaru ila-l-badle*). This rule places a great moral responsibility on experimenters and medical students to find alternatives.

The basic point to understand about using animals in science is that the same moral, ethical and legal codes should apply to the treatment of animals as are being applied to humans. According to Islam, all life is sacrosanct and has a right of protection and preservation.

The Holy Prophet Muhammad(s) laid so much emphasis on this point that he declared: "There is no man who kills {even} a sparrow or anything smaller, without its deserving it, but God will question him about it."

> Narrated by Ibn 'Omar and by Abdallah bin Al-As. An-Nasai, 7:206,239, Beirut. Also recorded by Musnad al-Jami - Ad-Darimi; Delhi, 1337. Also, Mishkat al-Masabih; English translation by James Robson, in four volumes; Sh. Muhammad Ashraf, Lahore, Pakistan; 1963 (hereafter referred to as 'Robson'.

He who takes pity {even} on a sparrow and spares its life, Allah will be merciful on him on the Day of Judgement.

Narrated by Abu Umama. Transmitted by Al-Tabarani.

FUR AND OTHER USES OF ANIMALS

There is a large-scale carnage of fur-bearing animals....to satisfy human needs, most of which are non-essential, fanciful, wasteful and for which alternative, humane products are easily available....The excuse that such things are essential for human needs is no longer valid. Modern technology has produced all these things in synthetic materials and they are easily available all over the world, in some cases at a cheaper price.

Some juristic rules that apply are: "That which was made permissible for a reason, becomes unpermissible by the absence of that reason." (*Ma jaza le uzrin, batala be zawalehi*) and "All false excuses leading to damage should be repudiated." (*Sadduz-zarae al-mua'ddiyate ela-l-fasad*). These rules leave no excuse for the Muslims to remain complacent about the current killing of animals in their millions for their furs, tusks, oil, and various other commodities.

The Qur'an does mention animals as a source of warm clothing (Qur'an 16:5), but modern-day clothing made of synthetic fibers is just as warm as clothing made from animal skins and makes clothing from animal skins unnecessary. The Qur'an refers only to the skins and furs of domesticated cattle which either die their natural death or are slaughtered for food. Today, millions of wild animals are killed commercially just for their furs and skins, while their carcasses are left to rot. Fourteen centuries ago Islam realized the absurdity of this wasteful and cruel practice and passed laws to stop it in the following Ahadith:

> The Holy Prophet Muhammad(s) prohibited the use of skins of wild animals.
>
> Narrated by Abu Malik on the authority of his father. Abu Dawud and Tirmidhi as recorded in Garden of the Righteous - Riyad as-Salihin of Imam Nawawi; translated by M.Z. Kahn; Curzon Press, London, 1975; [hereafter referred to as Riyad]; Hadith No. 815, p. 160.

The Holy Prophet Muhammad(s) forbade the skins of wild animals being used as floor-coverings. (id)

THE SAYINGS OF MUHAMMAD—OF ANIMALS AND DUTIES OWED THERETO BY SHIHAB AL-DIN AL-SUHRAWARDI (D. 1191)

"Are there rewards for our doing good to quadrupeds, and giving them water to drink?" Muhammad said, "Verily there are heavenly rewards for *any* act of kindness to a live animal."

Verily God hath one hundred loving kindnesses: one of which He hath sent down amongst man, quadrupeds and every moving thing upon the face of the earth: by it they are kind to each other, and forgive one another; and by it the animals of the wilds are kind to their young; and God hath reserved ninety-nine loving kindnesses, by which He will be gracious to His creatures on the last day.

A man came before the *Rasul* (messenger) with a carpet, and said, "O Rasul! I passed through a wood, and heard the voices of the young birds; and I took and put them into my carpet; and their mother came fluttering round my head, and I uncovered the young, and the mother fell down upon them, then I wrapped them into my carpet; and there are the young which I have." Then the Rasul said, "Put them down." And when he did so, their mother joined them: and Muhammad said, "Do you wonder at the affection of the mother towards her young? I swear by Him who hath sent me, verily God is more loving to His creatures than the mother to these young birds. Return them to the place from which ye took them, and let their mother be with them."

Once Ali was seated and a cat came and fell asleep upon the edge of his cloak. Lest he disturb the cat when he needed to leave, he cut the fabric of his coat around the sleeping cat.

Related by the Caliph Ali

***

FROM *ISLAM AND THE WONDERS OF CREATION: THE ANIMAL KINGDOM*
By Annemarie Schimmel,
Al-Furqan Islamic Heritage Foundation, London

"One of the most touching cat stories in early Arabic history relates the tale of the Sufi from Baghdad, Abu Bakr al-Shibli (d. 945) who died and was seen by one of his friends in a dream. On being asked what God had done to him, he said that he had been granted admission to Paradise but was asked by the Lord if he knew the reason for this blessing. Shibli enumerated all his religious duties — fasting and praying, performing the Pilgrimage and giving alms— but none of these acts of piety had saved him. Finally the Lord asked him, 'Do you remember the cold day in Baghdad when it was snowing and you were walking in your coat when you saw a tiny kitten on a wall shivering with cold, and you took it and put it under your warm coat? For the sake of this kitten We have forgiven you.'"

"There is a lovely story of the Prophet rescuing a gazelle. As he was out walking he saw that a gazelle had fallen into a trap. He talked to her and she told him that her two kids were waiting for her to feed them, but how could she reach them? The Prophet helped her out of the trap and promised to wait in her place until she had performed her motherly duties. While he was standing there the hunter arrived, deeply disappointed to see that his prey had gone and that a man (he did not know it was the Prophet) had taken her place. Then the gazelle came back accompanied by her kids, and the hunter, touched by this sight repented and not only let the gazelle go but embraced Islam. This story was so much loved that in the Sindhi language alone there are thirteen long poems dealing with this topic."

***

'Attar, *Tadhkirat al-Awliya*, Arberry translation as *Muslim Saints and Mystics*:

One day Abu Yazid [Bistami] was walking with a party of disciples. The road narrowed, and just then a dog approached from the opposite direction. Abu Yazid retired, giving the dog right of way.

The chance thought of disapproval occurred to one of the disciples. "Almighty God honored man above all other creatures. Abu Yazid is the 'king of the Gnostics' yet with all his dignity, and such a following of disciples, he makes way for a dog. How can that be?"

"Young man," Abu Yazid replied, "this dog mutely appealed to me: 'What shortcoming was I guilty of in the dawn of time, and what exceptional merit did you acquire, that I was clad in the skin of a dog whereas you were robed in honor as king of the Gnostics?' This was the thought that came into my head, so I made way for the dog."

One day Abu Yazid was proceeding along the way when presently a dog ran alongside him. Abu Yazid drew in his skirt. "You are not fit to travel with me and be my partner," the dog said, "For I am rejected of all men, whereas you are accepted of men."

"I am not fit to travel along with a dog," said Abu Yazid. "How shall I then travel along with the Etneral and Everlasting one? Glory be to that God, who educates the best of creatures by means of the least of creatures."

Ahmad Ghazali, *Sawanih*, Nasrollah Pourjavady translation:

One day Jesus and his disciples were walking in a narrow street, and they came up on a dead dog. The dog was decomposing, and the stench filled the whole alley. The disciples picked up their robes, tiptoed around the dead creature, and held their noses. Jesus knelt by the dog, and gazed at it lovingly. He said: "Praise be to God, what beautiful white teeth this creature had!"

The lover relates everything that is like the beloved to the beloved. Majnun had not had anything to eat for several days. He captured a deer; but instead of killing it he treated it gently and set it free. When asked for an explanation he said: "There is something in it which is like my Layla, and for a lover cruelty is not allowed."

***

LOVE THY ANIMALS
By Dr. Assad Nimer Busool
This article is adapted from the Animal Rights and
Ecology in the Islamic Educational Foundation of Illinois.

The teachings of the Qur'an and the traditions of the Prophet led Muslims regardless of their education and social status to be kind to animals. It is true that the Prophet Mohammed's (Peace be upon him) main concern was the welfare of this people; he indeed labored very hard to give them security and sustenence. And before his death, Muslims were secured and well-fed wherever they were. However, this concern extended to animals and the environment, too. Whenever he saw a weak, bruised, working or riding animal, he found its owner and asked him to take good care of his animal. One day, the Prophet entered a grove which belonged to one of the Ansars, and there he saw a camel. When the camel saw the Prophet, he moved toward him. Tears were flowing out of his eyes. The Prophet approached him, rubbed its head, and the camel calmed down. The Prophet asked, "Who is the owner of this camel?" A young man replied, "He belongs to me, O Messenger of God." The Prophet said, "Do you not fear God? Who gave you the ownership of this beast? He complained to me that you do not feed him and you overwork him." (Reported by Abu Dawud). Then the Prophet asked the camel's owner, "What are you going to do with your camel?" The man replied, "We want to slaughter him while he still has some flesh." The Prophet said "Don't do that. Sell him to me." The man answered, "He is yours, O Messenger of God." The Prophet sent him to graze with the Sadaqh camels until he died naturally (See Ibn Kathir-Shama'il ar-Rasul.)

Ahmad Ibn Hanbal reported that once Umar Bin Al-Khattab expressed his desire for a meal of fresh fish. His aide, Yarifa', without telling him, jumped on the back of one of Umar's camels and traveled for two nights going and two nights returning to buy a basket of fresh fish for Umar. When he arrived home, he washed the camel, but when Umar learned of what his aide did, he said to him, "Let me look at the camel first." He went to the camel and inspected it very closely. Suddenly he turned, saying, "You forgot to wash the sweat, and its ears. You tortured an animal to satisfy Umar's desires. By God, Umar will never taste the fish. Take your basket away from me."

A person who owns livestock must spend on them the provision that their kind requires, even if they have aged or become sick, so much that no benefit comes from them; he should not burden them beyond what they can bear; he should not put them together with anything by which they would be injured, whether of their own kind or other species, whether by breaking their bones or hurting or wounding; he should slaughter them gently and with kindness; he should not slaughter their young within their sight, but he should separate them; he should make comforable their resting and watering places; he should not discard those whom he takes for game; and neither shoot them with anything that breaks their bones nor causes their distruction by any means that renders their meat unlawful to eat.

BIOGRAPHIES

RABBI ANSON LAYTNER

Rabbi Anson Laytner is the executive director of the Seattle Chapter of the American Jewish Committee. Previously, from 1993 through 2004, he served as the executive director of Multifaith Works, a Seattle non-profit agency that provides low-income housing and emotional and practical support to people living with AIDS or other life-threatening illnesses. He also is an adjunct professor with Seattle University's Department of Theology and Religious Studies. In 1999, he was awarded a Hesselbein Community Innovation Fellowship with the Peter F. Drucker Foundation (now the Leader to Leader Institute). Prior to working at Multifaith Works, Laytner headed the Seattle Jewish Federation's Community Relations Council from 1982 to 1992. During this time, he helped found the Washington Association of Jewish Communities, the Interfaith Council of Washington, and the North American Interfaith Network.

As a volunteer, Laytner serves on the board of the Sino-Judaic Institute and edits its journal, Points East. In 2004, he was appointed to the King County Task Force on Human Services by County Executive Ron Sims. He has served on the boards of the Program for Early Parent Support (PEPS), the Northwest Development Officers Association, the Interfaith Alliance of Washington, the Coalition for a Jewish Voice, and many other non-profit organizations. He is a pastpresident of the Washington Coalition of Rabbis and the Interfaith Council ofWashington.

Laytner is the author of the cult classic *Arguing with God* (Jason Aronson, 1998) and over sixty articles on subjects ranging from Jewish theology to the Arab-Israel conflict to the Chinese Jews. His work-in-progress is a study of god-concepts and the meaning of suffering, entitled "Letting Go of God".

Laytner has a BA, summa cum laude, from York University in Toronto, a MA of Hebrew Letters and rabbinic ordination from Hebrew Union College, a Masters in Not-for-Profit Leadership from Seattle University, and an honorary Doctor of Divinity from Hebrew Union College. He is also a graduate of Seattle's Leadership Tomorrow program.

Rabbi Laytner is married to Merrily McManus Laytner, a development consultant. Between them, they share three daughters, two sons-in-law, and four grandkids.

RABBI DANIEL E. BRIDGE

Rabbi Daniel E. Bridge has been the Greenstein Family Executive Director of Hillel Foundation for Jewish Campus Life at the University of Washington since 1988. With degrees in German Language and Literature, Microbiology, Hebrew Letters, and a Certificate in Jewish Communal Service, Bridge has worked in both health care and Jewish community organizing. A past Assistant Director of the Pacific Southwest Council for Reform Judaism and past member of the California State Commission on the Changing Family, Rabbi Bridge has served on numerous local and national boards, including the Central Conference of American Rabbis. His two sons, Jacob and Zachary, are students at the University of California at Santa Cruz.

DR. SEYYED HOSSEIN NASR

Dr. Seyyed Hossein Nasr was born in 1933 in Tehran, Iran, into a family of educators and scholars, his father having been one of the founders of the Persian educational system. Consequently, he received the best classical Persian and Islamic education during his early years in Tehran. He later came to the West to finish his secondary education at the Peddie School in New Jersey and after graduating as the valedictorian of his class, he went to MIT where he studied physics and mathematics and graduated with honors in 1954. Meanwhile, his interest turned to an ever greater degree to philosophy and the history of science and he transferred to Harvard University to pursue graduate studies first in the field of geology and geophysics in order to acquaint himself with a descriptive as well as a mathematical science, and finally in the field of the history of science and philosophy in which he received his doctorate from Harvard University in 1958 with specialization in Islamic cosmology and science. From 1958 until 1979, he was professor of the history of science and philosophy at Tehran University and for several years the dean of the Faculty of Letters and for sometime the vice chancellor of the University. He also served for several years as president of Aryamehr University in Iran. In 1962 and 1965 he was visiting professor at Harvard University and in 1964-65 the first Aga Khan professor of Islamic studies at the American University of Beirut. He was also the founder and first president of the Iranian Academy of Philosophy.

In 1979 Dr. Nasr migrated to the United States where he became first the distinguished professor of Islamic studies at the University of Utah, then from 1979 to 1984 professor of Islamic studies at Temple University. Since 1984 he has been University Professor of Islamic studies at the George Washington University.

Dr. Nasr has lectured widely throughout the United States, Western Europe, most of the Islamic world, India, Australia and Japan. He has also given several major lectures such as the Azad Memorial Lecture in India, the Iqbal Lecture in Pakistan, the Charles Strong Memorial Lecture in Australia, the Gifford Lectures at the University of Edinburgh in Scotland and the Cadbury Lectures at Birmingham University in England. He has also been for ten years member of the directing committee of FISP (Federation Internationale des Societes Philosophiques) and a member of the Institut International de Philosophie.

Dr. Nasr is the author of over thirty books and over 300 articles. His works concern not only various aspects of Islamic studies but also comparative philosophy and religion, philosophy of art and the philosophical and religious dimensions of the environmental crisis.

KULSUM BEGUM

Born in the former princely city of Hyderabad in 1960, Kulsum (Kulthum in Arabic) hails from a family who had all turned to traditional Islamic and Indian art's commercial call to meet the needs of livelihood. Her father Mir Mahmood Ali (d.1984) had started his career writing number plates in the police service, only to give it up to learn and master the mysteries of miniature painting under Banaiyyah, the miniature painter by appointment to the court of the former ruler, the Nizam. With the disappearance of the princely states in India and a revolution in the people's life-styles, Banaiyyah had taken to teaching people of all ages in the interests of the preservation of his knowledge and art and with Government patronage, at a cottage industries centre for arts and crafts, where people produced and painted object d'art of wood, paper mache and pieces of ivory etc, all delicately hand painted with myriad folkloric and cultural themes under the label of Nirmal Industries, for these to be sold at Government emporiums in the country. The locality of Nirmal after which this industry was named had once been a major local regional centre for such traditional crafts.

After six years of training with Banaiyyah, Mahmood Ali was to work at Nirmal Industries for around 25 years thanks to the former's patronage while running an atelier of his own at home, in which all members of his family were involved. During the earlier years, "Wasl" (old paper pasted together in duplicate or triplicate using flour gruel, with the required thickness always in mind) would be scraped with a sharp knife after drying, and then polished with coral shells to provide the surface with the required smoothness. After the paper would be ready and cut to the wanted shape and size, if this had not already been done earlier, Mahmood Ali would proceed to draw or copy in pencil the subject or outline of the miniature and then, selecting the appropriate candidate to colour it, would explain the scheme in detail, along with how to produce the relevant shades and hues out of the twelve colours used, while for gold, a powder locally available would be utilised. Earlier on, colours prepared at home from natural substances like vegetables such as beetroot, pigments and pastes from plants, powdered minerals and precious and semi-precious stones would have been made use of.

When the introduction of calligraphy was required, the miniature would be taken at an early relevant stage to the calligrapher they dealt with, for him to copy down the required legend in Persian (the official language of India until the end of the 19th century), Ara-

bic and very rarely Urdu, as it was considered a latter day development and did not attain official status amongst Muslims till after
the derecognition of Persian. For themes rooted in Hindu cultural
and religious folklore, recourse would have been had to scribes well
versed in the Devanagri and the Telgu scripts. After the inclusion of
the relevant text, it would be covered with "Abari" ("clouds") en-
circling the script or other inter linear decoration. The last work on
the miniature would be the drawing of the borders and their illu-
mination or illustration. Keeping an ever watchful eye on the members of his atelier in the interests of the quality of their work and its
reputation in the market, Mahmood Ali would spend hours with
them in the house when not making deliveries, purchasing material or receiving fresh orders. For finer details, brushes he would
prepare with ten or twelve hairs of a squirrel's tail and with a tip
would be used, while for the purposes of lamination of painted
pieces of ivory, a coating of transparent glue would be daubed all
over in order to render the colours safe from smudging. It is said
that, such would be the diligence and level of devotion of each member of the atelier to his work that, each full-fledged member could
produce no less than five such standard paintings of commercial
quality a month, and almost double that number in times of crisis.
However, a good detailed painting always took its due course in
time and attention.

The product of such a school, regimen and work atmosphere, when
Kulsum was first discovered by Sultan Ghalib al-Qu'aiti in her early
teens, he had already known her father for some five years and was
amazed to notice that, not only had she greater gifts in miniature
painting than her father, but given sufficient time, and provided
the subject and theme of the miniature was explained to her clearly,
she could produce, despite her limited cultural scope, vision, educational limitations and tender years, as fine master pieces as some
of the best of the great masters of yore, but mostly by copying in
keeping with the requirements of the booked orders, without any
idea or care for her natural gifts.

In order to promote her and at least enable her to eke a better deal
out of her great talent for herself and her large family, particularly
after the demise of her father, Sultan Ghalib decided to take the
chance of introducing her to Her Royal Highness Princess Maha

Muhammad al-Faisal of Sa'udi Arabia, a genuine enthusiast of all things Islamic and a discreet supporter and promoter of Islamic culture, art and welfare work involving women and always keen to introduce her Sa'udi sisters to the art and cultured attainments of their Muslim fellow-beings in other parts of the world as an educational and motivational step.

Hence, since several years, Kulsum has been enjoying the patronage of Princess Maha, in Sa'udi Arabia, working at first with a handicapped Pakistani Calligrapher, Ustad 'Abdus Salam on Islamic art themes, and of late with others from the Philippines, in illuminating tales of mysterious wonder for audiences of all ages, authored by none other than the erudite and highly gifted Princess Maha herself; and they all deserve plaudits, not merely for their own rich talents, but also for their noble endeavours in playing the role of cultural ambassadors between the various wings of the Islamic lands in their own unique soft-spoken way, as also the rest of the world and in presenting a better practical explanation of the meaning as well as the dimensions of the cultural synthesis of Islam and its unique feature of adaptability. May we pray that the Almighty bless them and Grant them all success and always – 'Ameen'.

Sultan Ghalib al-Qu'aiti
Hyderabad, 14th August, 2004

BIBLIOGRAPHY

JUDAISM

Ecology & the Jewish Spirit: Where Nature and the Sacred Meet
by Bernstein, Ellen

L'Avdah u'l'shamra: A Jewish obligation to protect the environment
by Gersh, Akiva

The Jewish Sourcebook on the Environment and Ecology
by Isaacs, Ronald H.

Environment in Jewish Law: Essays and Responsa (Studies in Progressive Halakhah, 12)
by Jacob, Walter & Zemer, Moshe

Judaism and Animal Rights: Classical and Contemporary Responses
by Kalechofsky, Roberta

Judaism and Ecology (World Religions and Ecology Series)
by Rose, Aubrey

Judaism and Vegetarianism
by Schwartz, Richard H.

Judaism and Global Survival
by Schwartz, Richard H.

Garden of Choice Fruit: 200 Classic Jewish Quotes on Human Beings and the Environment
by Stein, David E.

Judaism and Ecology: Created World and Revealed Word (Religions of the World and Ecology)
by Tirosh-Samuelson, Hava

Torah of the Earth: Exploring 4,000 Years of Ecology in Jewish Thought
by Waskow, Arthur

ISLAM

Islam and Ecology : A Bestowed Trust (Religions of the World and Ecology)
by Foltz, Richard C. et al

GENERAL

Deep Ecology and World Religions: New Essays on Sacred Ground (S U N Y Series in Radical Social and Political Theory)
by Barnhill, David Landis et al

This Sacred Earth: Religion, Nature, Environment
by Gottlieb, Roger S.